MW00640149

THE LIGHT OF HOPE

C.N. Jannain

Copyright © 2018 C.N. Jannain

All rights reserved. No part of this book may be reproduced in any form or by any electronic or mechanical means including information storage and retrieval systems, without permission in writing from the author.

The only exception is by a reviewer, who may quote short excerpts in a review.

Printed in the United States of America

For more information on future works, events, and blogs visit:

Author Website: www.cnjannain.com
Book Website: www.thelightofhopebook.com
Facebook: C.N. Jannain
Twitter: @authorcnjannain
Instagram: @author_c.n.jannain

Cover Credit: Samsara Tamrakar

Library of Congress Control Number: 2018914096

Paperback ISBN: 9781732850903
EBook ISBN: 9781732850910

We are stars wrapped in skin,
The light you are seeking
has always been within.

I dedicate this book to my family
Who has always believed in me.

CONTENTS

CHAPTER ONE

Hope and Healing

They had her on a slab and ran their hands over her body. The group was comprised of six women around the girl, with a seventh nearby. Similar to a symphony, one would start and meet the second's hands. She would sweep toward the next woman. Women across from one another worked in the same manner.

The group stood in a peaceful clearing surrounded by a grove of trees. One heard the babbling brook, the sounds of the birds and the aroma of many flowers wafting across by the slow breeze. It looked like someone had swept the dirt floor of the circular clearing to create this space. Around the edges stood beautiful clay painted pots holding candles. Designs on the pots had meaning and offered boundaries and protection to the space. The edge outside this area grew thick with vegetation, some pine trees, and other sorts of plant life. The women chose this spot because of the pine trees that possess a unique energy and recharge all living things. Many flowers and berry bushes grew near the brook and in the small areas where sunlight penetrated the canopy.

The girl was in another worldly place. A cool cloth with salve on it soothed her wounds. In the circle to the side stood a big metal iron pot with a low fire under it. Steam rose as the Wise One tended to it.

The women had been there for many hours. The girl had many cuts and bruises. They would continue to work on her as long as needed, resting if possible. What they did not see on her insides they knew intuitively. The wisest of them led this special group. She was the leader of their village, their guide, and teacher. These women understood things of their world and the other world, the world beyond. After a long time of working on the girl, one woman at her feet reached under the slab and got a soft furry blanket from a basket and covered the girl. The Wise One who sat by the pot took care of other duties. With her, there was seven women. She seemed to be the one who took care of the important tasks, such as the fire. She had laid furs down on the ground, the order of everything here had importance. There were seven places for them when they all retired for the night. Once the girl healed, they would leave.

The seventh woman, the Wise One, came over to the girl after she dipped her thumb into a little dish of salve. She took it and put it across the spot on the forehead between the eyebrows. Earlier, she put a pot on the fire with some water for a broth to strengthen the women and to nourish their bodies. She added healing herbs in it and some root vegetables and beans. They didn't eat meat in this place. They used beans and other foods for their protein. The women worked many hours over the girl.

After the woman put the salve on the girl's forehead and brushed her long dark hair away from her face and stroked her cheek lovingly, she stood there. She looked upward and closed her eyes, then down at the girl; the women did the same. She spoke, a prayer of some sort. When she finished, she looked into each woman's eyes. All the women had deep brown eyes and long dark hair. Their facial features and the details of their bodies defined them. The Wise One gave a signal with a gaze. They stepped back and away. It was time to rest and nourish their bodies.

The women seemed to understand where to go and which spot belonged to them. They turned and walked to the furs and sat down. Silence permeated the air. It was almost sundown. The seventh woman, the Wise One's name was Gracemama. She walked over to the cooking area within the circle where there were primitive bowls and spoons and took a hand carved ladle and filled the bowls with healing and nutritious broth. Gracemama served each woman before herself. They ate, being mindful of the food, the flavor, and gaining all the strength they could from it. They chewed their food well, mashing it with their teeth into a liquid. From a young age they had learned to eat this way.

They observed the girl's chest rising and falling. She was breathing peacefully. In contrast, the girl's mind raced with thoughts. Why was she running through a wheat field? Her heart pounded. The girl did not grasp what she ran from except that it felt like fear itself. Her legs burned, but she didn't want to stop. She ran as fast as her body would go. Propelled ahead, she realized something helped her, pushed her to keep going. The sun beat down

3

on her, beads of sweat ran down her face and body. Her sweat soaked her clothes. She saw a village up ahead. She wondered how long she could continue running at this pace because of exhaustion. The girl's instructions were to travel in the direction she was but she couldn't remember why or what she was running from. She reached the perimeter of the village. Some wouldn't notice the village and would walk right past it. This was the work of the wise woman. If someone needed to be there, they would find it. She crossed the outskirts of the village and could see a few women watching her. She didn't have time to register the details of what she saw when she fell to the ground with exhaustion. Then her mind went blank. She had lost consciousness.

As she lay on the slab, this recording played in her mind repeatedly. The girl remembered nothing beyond falling to the ground. She knew she felt fear and ran from something, but wasn't sure what. Did she even want to know? Eventually, her mind became quiet. Her being rested. It had connected with all the others that slept.

In contrast to the girl's recurring dream or vision, the night and surroundings here were silent and peaceful. This place seemed protected.

The women sat and ate their broth and seemed to eat in this rhythm of connectedness. They would savor the taste, chewing, and gaining strength. Each woman sat in a cross-legged position on her spot. Then again like a dance, they seemed to move into prayer. Gracemama was leading the rhythm. The women understood when to shift. After finishing their food and Gracemama collecting the bowls, she returned to her spot and picked up a drum. As she started a beat, she matched the rhythm with words.

It moved into a melody. Each woman had a small drum on their bedding. They picked them up and played. Each one taking their turn. When they stopped, Gracemama played a graceful ending before putting her instrument down. The women sat quietly. Then in unison, they lay down, and all drifted off to sleep.

The sun had gone down, and the women covered up for warmth. It was a cool spring night. The women slept. The girl was still, just a quiet breath on the slab. She was in another place.

CHAPTER TWO

The Region

The village that Hope had run to before she collapsed looked like this. Two circles of dwellings surrounded a huge hall in the middle for activities like gatherings of any sort. The outer circle took care of the inner circle as these housed the teachers and wise women.

People in the village had various tasks such as cooking, weaving, carving, and gardening. Each dwelling had a large yard surrounding it with individual personalities. The cooking area had a nearby table for meals with shelves for utensils, plates, bowls and pots to cook with. Herbs hung from one pole to another to dry. Stools stood around the table and a work bench nearby. There were only women, no children running around.

Off and away from the village were cliffs, mountains and caves. This was a special place used for specific learning, vision quests or quiet. It might serve as a place of renewal for some. There were hot water springs one could soak in and detoxify, whatever needed to be, relieve achy muscles, or just cleanse. If someone traveled there for that purpose often they would stay a few days. One cave belonged to the keeper of the caves, the wise woman Gracemama, who helped Hope. In her cave, she kept many herbs and flowers, which she used for healing. This is often where a lot of teaching and training for the women who helped her with Hope took place.

The young girl was healing in a protected area away from the village. Women stood way off around the area to create a protected perimeter around the sacred circle. The sentries stood throughout the surrounding woods while the seven women worked on Hope. They stood stationed to keep guard and to control access to this place. They had developed a sensitivity to anything around them. Animals, except those invited, would not enter because they knew not to pass. The path leading in and out was obscure. It was wide enough to walk on but had thick vegetation hiding it on either side.

Gracemama led this group of healers. Born and raised into her role she now had great wisdom with her years. She trained to do this work many, many years ago.

This group comprised seven women. The number seven is a most sacred and special number. Some meanings of the number seven are the seeker, the thinker, and the searcher of truth. The number seven means take nothing at face value. It is always trying to understand the underlying hidden truths. Seven understands nothing is as it seems and often an illusion.

Others learned and trained. They did not become apart of this group until they earned it. The students did not go here. Gracemama would choose a replacement if someone left the group. They had to be ready and exceed the basic training. Occasionally, an eighth person joined. They would be a part of the leader who trained them, so invisible to the count. Gracemama would come and go. Sometimes she would live in the village. When she needed quiet or to teach someone or other reasons of her own she would go to the caves.

Before sunrise, the healing circle rested in the quiet. Gracemama's head popped up. She looked over at the healers and saw no activity. She looked at the girl and noticed the slightest twitch in her fingers. The twitch spread to her hands. The girl made the tiniest movement. Gracemama sat up and beat a steady low rhythm on her drum. The women lifted their heads up. Next, they came to a sitting position. Finally, they stood. They all walked over to the girl and took the same spots they had the previous day. They laid their hands on her body, ankles, hips, and shoulders. Gracemama put her drum down and headed over to the girl. She cupped her cheeks in a comforting warm way. The girl displayed movement. She appeared calm. The girl tried to move her fingers and wiggle her toes. They saw her movements under the blanket.

Gracemama walked over to the pot of salve and brought it back to the table and set it on the ground. The girl opened her eyes as the women rolled down the blanket. They removed the blanket and then the bandages. The girl remained quiet and still. Healing salve passed around the group, and each woman put a little in her hands. The wounds had disappeared. The women massaged her legs and arms with the creme. After they finished, they covered the girl with a light blanket and just held the energy around the girl. She tried to speak but no sound came out. She lay and rested for a while. As time passed, she wanted to move more, and she did. The women just observed her to keep her safe. Eventually, she wanted to sit up. The three women at her head and shoulders helped her to sit up and swing her legs around so they would hang. As she sat up she experienced lightheadedness but didn't want to lie back down again.

Gracemama filled a bowl with broth; nothing else, just the liquid and brought it to the girl. She spooned it into the girl's mouth. The girl sipped. She appeared hungry. After the broth, the girl seemed a little better. Gracemama helped her get down from the table and to her spot.

They sat on Gracemama's blanket together. The girl had a light blanket around her. Gracemama pulled out a dress from a basket, and she helped the girl put it on, and removed the blanket. She then took a primitive comb out of the basket and combed her hair. The girl smiled. This was comforting and familiar. The girl didn't understand why she couldn't speak or where she was. She remembered the dream, but then it stopped at some point. She tried to speak again and couldn't. The Wise One made a shushing sound. She was signaling the girl not to talk.

They all spent one more night there. The girl slept next to the Wise One and seemed comforted by her warmth. When the sun rose, everyone ate porridge and packed up. Once everyone packed they put their satchels on their backs. Gracemama gave the girl one she packed for her. It was light, so she lifted it and put it on her back. It was early morning and cool. Gracemama gave the girl a woven shawl to keep her warm and cozy.

There was a hidden path out of the circle. It looked narrow but wide enough for two people to be on it side by side. Gracemama led them out. She took the girl's hand while they walked. Six of the women walked in a single line behind them. They walked at a mellow pace to begin with. Shrubbery grew on either side of the path; similar to a tunnel with no roof, only the sky above. The girl looked around with curiosity. After walking for some time, they passed a sentinel. Here, the path popped out of a hiding place through the bushes. They stepped through an opening in the shrubbery. It was a hidden doorway. They knew if one turned their body sideways they could slip through. The girl watched Gracemama then did the same, and so did the remaining six. When they emerged the path appeared much wider. When everyone had come through, and they walked a few steps, the girl glanced backward and did not see where they had come from. Once they came out into the open sky, she saw only their group. The women knew where to go. Everyone relaxed, walking in their normal stride. The women engaged in conversation. She heard occasional laughter behind her. These women were friends.

Gracemama would not go back to her cave, she would return to the village with everyone. She had a hut there that was hers. Gracemama and the girl would stay there for now. She was the keeper of the girl and would make sure she was all right; there were plans for the girl later. Gracemama would teach and train her. Everyone walked in a group, their mood more social now. Gracemama was in a very peaceful state, she wasn't like the other women, even when they came out of the area they had left behind.

She continued to hold the girl's hand and walked at a nice pace. They walked for a long time.

The sky appeared as a beautiful shade of blue. They traveled through an open grassy area with trees off in the distance. The group seemed to know where they were going but the path had disappeared. As they moved on they entered a more thickly grown area of trees, with less light and then it changed again. Further down the path trees grew but not as thick; the sunlight could come through and felt good on their bodies.

The group came upon the babbling brook where they stopped and took a break. Everyone sat down. They had some kind of container that held a special tea and some nuts. Everyone munched on nuts, then each individual got up and milled around. The women picked berries off of small shrubs by the brook. A woman walked over to the girl and Gracemama. She motioned to the girl to open her hands. She gave them some berries.

The girl couldn't believe the burst of flavor as she put one berry in her mouth and it burst open as she bit down. Once eaten, the woman gave her more. Her face lit up with a big smile. The girl tried to thank the woman, but no words came out. Gracemama knew when something traumatic happened, sometimes you would lose a sense or an ability. She hoped the girl's speech would return.

They all sat for a while and just relaxed and enjoyed the nature sounds. The brook was soothing. Everyone laid down and rested. Once they heard the signal of one clap from Gracemama, they understood to get up and walk again. Everyone was in tune. The clap was all they needed to rise. They walked until the sun went down looking for their campsite.

11

The women found the flat hidden area to camp off the trail. When they entered it, the women and Gracemama all laid down their ground coverings and bedding. Gracemama made a spot for herself and the girl. The girl watched. The women moved in rhythm with one another. Gracemama walked out of the circle to a tree. The girl observed her. She removed leaves and dirt at the bottom of the tree and then some wood that covered a hole. A box in the hole contained a pot and some basic food supplies. A select group from the village had put it there. They took care of this chore whenever necessary.

Gracemama started a fire after sending the women to collect dry wood. She again made a broth with beans and dried vegetables that re-hydrated with the liquid. This soup tasted different. Gracemama put different herbs and spices in it. It was delicious and nourishing. After eating, they all laid down to sleep. Tomorrow would be a long walk, and they would arrive home late. The women took turns putting wood on the fire throughout the night to keep them all warm. Everyone slept through the night.

As the sun came up, there was again a clap. The girl already knew what this sound meant and rose on her own along with everyone else. She felt like her senses were in tune to what was around them and to the women. She wished she could speak. They packed up and left. The box containing the cooking pot went back to its hidden spot after some porridge, and they left the camp as though no one had ever been there. They came out of the secluded spot and were back on the path. They walked for what seemed hours. The group seemed to pull each other along. At midday, they stopped to have food and a nice rest. Then they were on their way again.

Late in the afternoon, they passed an area of rocks and cliffs with caves. If one was close enough, a person might see the caves. With distance, they would not. This was where Gracemama lived when she came to the special caves. They hurried by and didn't stop. Everyone had to keep going to make it home. Gracemama's plan, was to take the girl to the village for integration into her new environment.

CHAPTER THREE

Heading Out

As the sun set off in the distance, the women caught sight of the smoke rising. They noticed something resembling dwellings. Soon the village came into view and the women acknowledged their destination up ahead.

The women of the village saw them coming. The girl made out a birdcall, and more women appeared. They stood on either side of the path while the group returned. They said nothing. The group walked through the tunnel of women and headed to one dwelling. Gracemama did not want to overwhelm the girl, she remained fragile from the events that brought her to them.

The six women dispersed once Gracemama and the girl settled in their own dwelling. Gracemama integrated the girl into her dwelling by giving her bedding right near her along the wall and a sitting place. She thought the girl would be more at home this way. The girl looked around and noted herbs hanging in one corner, and containers with various items in them. In the middle of the dwelling a

14

fire pit and a tripod stood. A pot hung from the tripod for cooking. As the sun set, the wood burned in the fire pit to create warmth. A curtain hung at the door for privacy and warmth. The girl appeared tired after she ate. She walked over to her spot that Gracemama set up for her. She lay down and drifted off to sleep.

The next day, they remained in the dwelling. Someone would bring them food and beverages. The Wise One wanted to keep her secluded for a little while. She didn't want to overload her senses. Gracemama did things such as sitting in meditation and singing soft sounds. She would move around and do tasks in the hut with the herbs. She made healing teas for the girl. This would assist the girl in her recovery from the trauma she experienced. Nightfall arrived, and they slept.

The next morning, the six women came to their place. The girl became familiar with them. Gracemama began a melody, which she sang over the past two days. All the women returned to that space of being as one. The girl liked the melody and would try to join in. Odd sounds came out. Her voice became the tiniest bit clearer. The girl didn't sing in a normal voice. The women and the Wise One smiled at her effort. Improvement would all happen in its own natural time. She understood this from the women. She realized this group of women intended to keep her safe and protected.

Someone brought food in the afternoon, and they all ate together. The mood became light, with smiles and laughter. When the sun set, Gracemama clucked her tongue three times. They seemed to have different signals for various purposes. The language remained unfamiliar for now, but she learned the signals. At that point, the women stood up and left. Gracemama gave the girl some tea, and then they both lay down for the night to go to sleep.

The next day, as the sun came up, Gracemama arose and they got ready for the day. They ate, washed up, and changed clothes. Gracemama gave the girl a long dress to wear. Embroidery of flowers appeared around the neckline and at the bottom of the sleeves. The beige dress incorporated little blue flowers with red centers. She received a shawl to keep her warm.

Gracemama pulled the curtain aside, the sun shone in. The girl put her hands over her eyes for a moment to block out the brightness of the sun. They headed to the door. With no one in sight, quiet permeated the space. Gracemama walked out of the door and waved her to follow. She gave the girl a tour so she would get her bearings.

After the tour around the village, the six other women joined them. They returned to Gracemama's place. They began different activities outside around the side of the hut. This area included different work areas for different purposes. One woman wove; two worked with the herbs, and so on. Gracemama appeared to be directing them. Their daily routine started like this. Gracemama gave specific instructions to the others on how to integrate the girl. She needed time and patience.

The weather remained pleasant as the day began with blue skies and comfortable temperatures. She shed her shawl on a sitting stool as the sun shone on her shoulders and back, warming her. The day progressed, and the girl enjoyed spending time with the women as they created various dishes. They encouraged her to join in and she did.

The girl spoke a few words and also realized the women comprehended her thoughts. She understood their dialect now. Gracemama assisted her with that.

They all worked for quite a while preparing the food and other tasks. A delicious aroma rose from the soup which gave off a sweet, delicious fragrance. The girl became hungry. One woman got off her stool and walked to a shelving area. She retrieved bowls and utensils carved from wood. They took down what they needed; and with a few trips took them over to a counter area. Then once again a clap, clap, and clap. The women put down their tasks and gathered in a line near the cooking pot. One woman served Gracemama who sat in her spot. She waited while everyone else in the line served themselves. They served the girl; she carried her own bowl and sat down. After a blessing over the food, they ate.

The girl studied the women eating and mimicked them. She found the food delicious. The women returned to their huts to rest. Gracemama and the girl rested too.

The girl realized time eluded her here. The sun rose and the sun set. That was her only guide. How long had she been here she wondered? Hope realized the women worked in unison when together doing a task. She found this predictable, something she could count on similar to a rhythm to their day.

When her eyes opened after resting one day, she sat up and took a little time on her sleeping area, Gracemama seemed to do the same. Then Gracemama returned to her cooking area and poured tea for them. She handed her a little sliver of wood with the bark removed and showed her how to chew the sliver. The wood tasted of peppermint, a flavor she recalled. Her breath became fresh, and she became more alert, its effect calmed her stomach similar to a digestive aide. She chewed the sliver until it became soft and then tossed it into the fire like Gracemama did.

When they rose, they joined the others for more activities. When the sun set, they slept. Many days passed like this, the girl grew to recognize the pattern. Hope walked from woman to woman learning different tasks and about their group. She became part of their heartbeat. Now she seemed safe and knew the pattern and little by little within the group they gave her responsibility.

Gracemama, her teacher, directed how things should go within the day and who she should work with. Hope learned new information everyday. Gracemama taught her how to use herbs. The girl tried to talk and mostly made sounds, but she possessed the ability to hear the women in her mind, which she found interesting. The funny thing is, she thought she remembered being here. That memory came from the day she ran here and collapsed. The villagers had left to integrate the girl with no fear or anxiety. Gracemama wanted it to be a peaceful transition. Gracemama told them she would tell them when to return.

The days continued the same more or less with a few variations. Then, one day, a group of women came back to the village, soon more returned. One day the girl walked over to Gracemama who put her hand on her head and reassured her. That day they visited various dwellings, some which the girl had not yet entered. Late one afternoon, around mealtime, the other women came over and shared a meal together. The girl looked around. Everyone in this group had similar long dark hair, dark eyes and tanned skin from being in the outdoors. They all smiled at her as she looked around.

After the meal, everyone returned to their dwellings and rested. Later, they all came out of their dwellings. It was a new moon, new beginnings, a time of celebration and ceremony. A big fire burned. All the women gathered. Each person owned a drum. The women sat on the ground on furs and Gracemama started the beat. Then the woman next to her, then the next like the domino effect. The girl had a part which Gracemama helped her with. After a while, the beat changed into a melody. One woman stood up with a bowl and spoon. She beat it and made her own rhythm. Others played to balance and make a melody with this new sound. Another woman stood up and held two carved sticks she beat together, then a morocco type instrument. At the end, a woman stood in the center with a wooden flute. The music sounded sweet, like a bird singing. Everyone supported each other in the melody with their instruments. It touched the young girl. She cried. Hope did not understand why. She did not have the ability to stop. Gracemama held her as she sobbed. It seemed like she was letting go of something. Something deep and painful she failed to remember. This sweet sound brought it out, but also comforted her with its beauty and love. A long time passed, and the music continued until the girl stopped and curled up in Gracemama's lap. She fell asleep, exhausted and spent as the music came to a close.

The woman who played the wooden flute came over picked up the girl and carried her to the hut. Hope did not wake. The women understood that the girl entered a dream state to travel and learn. Memories of what came before she had come here. She slept for many days. Her thoughts had her body jerking sometimes, speaking in her sleep, sweating. The flute lady, who trained for what the girl experienced now, stayed with her and took care of her. Gracemama had other duties. The state she was in would help her heal. Hope needed to go through this experience. Gracemama left the camp and returned to the caves. The flute lady stayed with the girl and did not leave her. Women brought her food. She would get broth into the girl's mouth, but not wake her. Hope needed the nourishment. They had been building her up for this journey. Gracemama believed the girl could heal in this induced dream state. The girl's body jerked and moved. In her mind she ran through a big huge field of wheat. It seemed like forever. She ran from a place she never wanted to return to. The girl experienced a darkness she had never felt before. The people in it appeared unkind and hurtful, without a soul. She had a flash of faces, familiar faces.

She experienced fear; it settled in her stomach area. She looked at the face of a man. This man looked angry and unsettled. He did not have a happy look or peace on his face. The man seemed familiar. Next to him lay a bottle, which he gripped, as he sat slumped against the wall. Others walked or sat around him. They appeared lifeless. The girl wondered if the empty bottle put him in this state. He looked lifeless like the others, no hope showed on his face. Was he further gone than the others? It saddened her. She sensed a thick grayness here. Like moving through sludge, heavy and burdensome. She did not like what she saw. She exited this place through a door. Outside, more grayness. People walked around, but they did not look happy, as if in a trance. There were women and men, and some children. A little blonde girl appeared. Hope recognized a clearness about her face even though she had a hood pulled close around her face. She saw enough. When she spotted the girl, she gave her the slightest smile. She walked with a woman, and they hurried. The village had stores and buildings. People lived here. Hope could not put her finger on it, this village seemed familiar. The place made her uncomfortable. However, she was here in the dream state and possessed the ability to see. There were various types of dream states. She continued to look around and entered many buildings. The thick grayness permeated the homes that people lived in. Everything seemed dull and lifeless. As she moved around, she would find the slightest light on one or two women's faces. She did not find this on any of the men so far. She entered another store and when she exited and looked up; she realized no sunshine appeared anywhere in the sky. What was this place? Why was she here? The man she first saw seemed familiar. She wondered where she knew him from. She continued to walk through the town wandering.

Hope entered a narrow road that incorporated cobblestone on it. The road would have been beautiful if clean, instead it appeared dull, with trash scattered everywhere. She continued on the street for quite a while. She came to a door on the left. The door appeared dingy like everything else. Hope saw a spot on the door where there was a little hatch to open from the inside. The girl noted simple cast iron bars across a little window in the door so that no one could reach in, but one possessed the ability to see out. This door looked familiar and if polished would be beautiful. Unfortunately it looked dingy. Planks of wood that made up the door contained great detail and history in them. The door handle was special. The knob had a familiar touch. She caught a glint and shine to it for a moment. She stood there for a long time and wanted to knock, but why? Next she put her hand up to do so and then dropped it. She left and continued on her walk.

At the end of this street, she came into a large circle area; it looked like it had the makings of a park. The play area had swings, a climbing area and a sandbox. The swings looked broken, the climbing structures rusty, and the sandbox had shovels and buckets stuck in hard crusty sand. This had been a play park for children. Dead leaves and grass appeared on the ground, the trees were no better. The park required a lot of cleaning up. A few children walked in the area, but they seemed dull and lifeless, with little talking and no laughter. Any talking sounded like a recording, no life to it, no tone, no intonations. People around the general area seemed to walk without purpose, some seemed to live on the street, and the homes were shoddy. People moved through the motions without purpose.

Everywhere the girl traveled, she continued to sense this. She appeared caught in a maze and panicked. Again the question why was she here in this place? She seemed trapped in it. It held some distant memory. The panic rose. Her forehead and palms became sweaty. The girl's heart pounded and her face grew pale. She ran, where she didn't know. Then she recognized a street and headed down it. Her exhaustion overtook her. She sensed hopelessness all around. It crept in and affected her. Right then she saw the doorknob, it was a shiny doorknob, glowing like she should spot it. She ran toward it. When she got there, she recognized the door that had caught her attention. She stopped, caught her breath, perceived the slightest glimmer of hope, but did not know why.

She collapsed right outside the door. In her mind's eye, she saw herself, but she had no more energy to rise. The place took over. In the quietest of sounds, she heard the door open with a slight creak. She saw someone looking at her. The eyes were blue and remarkable. They shone like jewels. Then she heard someone call, "mama, mama." The next thing she knew the door opened just enough and a woman and a girl; the girl she had spotted walking outside before, grabbed her arms and dragged her through and into the dwelling.

Once inside the door, she inhaled a big loud gasp for air. The air felt different in here. She lay on the floor and calmed. It took a while, then she sat up crossed legged on the floor and looked around. She appeared better but didn't understand why. As she looked around, she saw the room she was in had light. The things in the room were clean and sparkled. None of the energy and gray dullness of the outside appeared in here. She experienced confusion where was she? The funny thing was it seemed familiar, but she failed to figure it out. As she looked up, she saw the girl. Blonde hair, about her size, and age it seemed. Her blue eyes sparkled, and in here she was full of life and energy. She was silent, studying the girl while the girl studied her. The girl liked her; she was familiar. The girl seemed to have a light within that shone, and it appeared strong and good. The girl with the blue eyes pulled up a soft rug, and they sat across from each other and gazed at each other for a long time. She looked around for the woman who had helped pull her in the door. She was not there; the girl figured out she had left.

Both girls saw familiarity in their features. They looked alike except for the dark hair, eyes, and skin, to the fair blonde, blue eyes and light skin. The girls might be the same age; they were of similar build. The blonde girl smiled. She seemed more relaxed. She spoke, and it was in a language they both understood. "You are my sister. My twin." The girl's eyes got very large, and she sat digesting this statement. Something seemed familiar about the girl. "You escaped this place, we planned it together with our mother. Only one of us had the ability to go. You were weaker and needed to leave. I am stronger right now. We planned it over a long period." The girl asked what is this place. The blonde girl said, "A place where darkness is taking over, and it is our home. In here is one of the few places left where we have kept the light." "Who are you?" the girl asked. The blonde girl answered, "I am your sister, we are twins. We practiced before you left so you possessed the ability to return to us. You learned to go to sleep, and dream, and then transport your body to another place. You are dreaming to travel back to your home." This overwhelmed the girl. She tried to assimilate all this as she possessed no memory of it. Is this true, is this possible? The blonde girl had patience. They sat for a long time.

"You must eat to keep strong," said the sister. "But I am in a dream state?" stated the girl. "You are in a kind of dream state. We learned to travel this way so we can be together. As sisters we have a strong bond. We are sisters and twins.", said the sister. The girl gulped she found this too much to take in. Dream state, traveling, being somewhere else. The blonde girl got up and got a grain and bean dish. She handed a bowl to her sister, and they both ate. The girl seemed better after some food. How can I be eating? How am I here? The blonde girl read her thoughts, she said, "Yes you are here." "What is your name?" the girl said. "My name is Faithsister. Your name is Hopesister. But we can call each other Faith and Hope."

"It's been a long day, and you may be here a while, so let's get rest?" Hope asked, "Where is our mother you spoke of?" "She was here when we pulled you in, helped you get here, now she is out chasing the darkness away as much as she can. Our mother has power." Hope wondered what that meant. There were three wooden beds like cots with woven blankets. Faith took her bed, and pointed to another one the same size and said, "That's yours."

When the girls laid down for the night Hope just slept, she had no thoughts, no dreams tonight. In the morning she heard the little pitter-patter of feet and opened her eyes. Hope saw Faith cooking. The food smelled good, Hope's stomach rumbled. Why was she so hungry? As she woke up, Hope looked around. It was a simple home. There were a few very comfortable looking chairs in the corner with a small table. It was a place to relax or talk. Over by the cooking area, there was a round table with chairs to eat at. The floor had coverings. There were also two doors on the wall near the sitting corner. She wondered where they went. Faith looked over at her as she made food and smiled at her. Hope smiled back. She felt safe here and trusted Faith. She meant her no harm, she was caring for her.

Clean clothes laid on the end of her bed. Faith pointed to the door on the right as if to say you can go in there to change. She did. Hope walked into the small area, she found a pitcher and a bowl, a towel, a cloth, and a comb. There was soap and something familiar and minty tasting. Hope knew she should rub this on her teeth and then chew on it. This seemed a familiar ritual to her, and she knew what to do. Next she washed up and combed her hair, then put on the clothes, which fit. Hope appeared refreshed when she walked out of the small room. She walked over to the table and sat down and watched her sister. Faith seemed sure of herself. She had the ability to take care of herself and others if needed. Faith brought a bowl over which looked delicious. There were foods in the bowl she didn't recognize, and some herbs and spices. The aroma was familiar. It was colorful and alive. She sat down after giving each of them their bowls and tea, and they ate. Faith prayed over the food; Hope did the same. The food tasted amazing. How did someone so young know how to cook so well? She realized the food strengthened her body.

Faith talked a little to tell her what was going on. Her sister didn't tell her too much as she didn't want to overwhelm her. Faith said the food needed to be fresh to nourish them and keep them strong because of the dark forces outside. She said the darkness was spreading everywhere and her home was one of the few havens.

Their mother had a gift of bringing light to darkness. Her constant task was to keep the darkness out of their village. Sometimes she left for many days. There were a few more people like her, but she was the strongest, and Faith and Hope were a part of that. Faith explained her mother had sent Hope away. She told her to run to her destination as fast as she could so that the darkness failed to catch her. Her instructions, to go to Gracemama to learn skills to help save the village. Faith and Hope as twins were so connected. Faith would stay back with her mom. Hope would travel back to them through dreaming. She had the ability to be in two places at once. Right now her physical body was there with her sister, and a shell of her body was back at where Gracemama and the women lived.

Hope needed to have complete trust of the women in the village and learn as much as possible from them. She was to be the keeper of that knowledge and when she learned enough, come back to help them chase the darkness away.

Faith was stronger than Hope at the moment, and had what she needed to stay with her mom, but Hope's assignment was to learn much and maybe one day teach Faith. If all else failed, and it was still possible, Faith could join her sister. It was very important to keep the light alive. Faith stopped, that was enough for now, she trusted that Hope believed what Faith shared. She knew when the time had come to go on her journey, she might forget things, maybe everything. That was why it was so important to have her here now for a while. The women where she had gone knew all this because their mother had lived there a long time ago and could also travel as Hope had done. Her mother traveled to Gracemama to ask for help and to send Hope when the village became covered in darkness.

The girls enjoyed the rest of the morning together just talking and sharing about everything going on here and where Hope was with the women. She would understand everything in time. Faith thought they should go out. Hope could experience what was happening. They wouldn't stay long.

They drank vibrant life-giving tea and then put on capes with hoods to cover their bodies and their light. It was what her sister was wearing when she was out in the village before they had met. Hope had noticed a sliver of light through her sister's covering. She pulled her cape and hood closed this would keep her light from being seen. She would not stand out from the others. The tea they drank made their light stronger, but this was on purpose so that the darkness would not affect them as much. They headed out.

The darkness seemed as thick as soup outside, it was getting worse. Hope didn't like it. She didn't like the way it made her feel. It was difficult to move. They walked toward where Hope had first arrived. The man she had noticed at first when she arrived was there slumped down on the ground. He seemed impervious to his surroundings. Hope spoke to her sister. Her first words were, "Is he our Father?" Then Faith explained how the darkness had affected their Father. She explained that he would enjoy going out to drink at establishments and meet up with his friends. He had been a strong man, but the energy was lower in these places, and when the darkness came in, he wasn't strong enough to resist it. Mother didn't see it right away, and by the time she did along with everything changing in the village, it had taken her father, he did not have the ability to resist it. Mother couldn't save him from this. It broke her heart. Faith had the gift to see the tiniest spark still there, and she knew what a good man her Father had been. Faith wanted to help him, as did her mother, but they could not. She was still very much a student as was her sister. Faith wasn't strong enough yet in her skills. They walked on, and as they did, Faith told her how the darkness had crept in. It was slow and methodical. Darkness was tricky, sneaky; it had a life of its own. Hope now realized the enormity of it.

They walked on, and as they did, Faith told her everything. The whole city had been so full of the light. It began when some travelers were passing through town. There was a drinking and food place they would hang out. They were cunning. These folks brought the darkness. They had done this before. Far away from here, they had taken down other villages. They would chat up with the locals and drink and be merry, but their intentions were pure darkness. And the drinking establishments was the perfect environment. They began by influencing people to make bad choices they sugar-coated with lies. The darkness targeted the weakest at first, and then it spread. Once everyone had realized what had happened, it was too late. It took over everything except for a handful who lived and helped like Mother. The other towns didn't have such powerful people who could rid the town of darkness. That is why they had sent Hope off to help and save the village. She would be primary in this. She did not understand the power she would wield yet. The darkness took on a life of its own and took more of the villagers in.

Hope was sensing darkness, her sister was more used to it and the signs, and how to protect herself and when to go home. Faith noticed Hope weakening a little, so they headed home. Hope noticed that as they came toward the house, it was like a beacon. When they touched the doorknob to go in, it was like a cleansing. Faith showed Hope, she had not noticed this when she first came in, but now she did. When she touched the handle, she felt better.

This was the power of her mother. She had set this up with some of her light infused into the handle. Mother could do this with other things. The girls entered their home and put their cloaks in a basket with a lid. They did not want the energy spreading. They needed to keep them the way they were so they could go out without being noticed. Hope was glad to be inside.

The twins headed to the sitting area, Faith got up and made some kind of drink to cleanse them further. She sweetened it, it was delicious. Hope was back to normal. She looked around the room. Hope noticed someone on Mother's bed. Faith nodded knowing her thoughts. The woman was sleeping with blankets piled on her and a scarf over her head. She could see dark hair coming out, but that was all. It was getting late. The girls ate something, then went to bed. Hope wondered how long she would be here.

CHAPTER FOUR

Experiencing Darkness

Back where her body was in a dream state, or travel state, the women kept vigil over her. These women received training to make sure nothing happened, and that Hope returned safely. Hope would return in time, and the women would sit as long as necessary often in shifts as the days passed. She traveled to her village for a reason. She needed to understand why.

When Hope awoke, her mother had left. Her work remained extremely important to the occurrences and any chance of righting things. The girls continued to go out over the days and weeks that followed. Faith wanted to get Hope in shape like a marathon runner. She wanted her out in the muck so she would become strong and would resist the darkness better. These exercises held a purpose. She would find out the reason later. As Hope grew stronger, the darkness did not affect her as much. Each trip became easier. They walked by the spot her father occupied every day. He did not recognize them. This made the girls sad. Engulfed by darkness, except for a tiny place, which might be the father's saving grace. Faith would enter and leave stores and restaurant/bars and make sure her sister kept her light strong. It was a slow process of staying in that moment and holding love for whatever kept her grounded in her light. Love seemed to be a huge piece of this process. When she went out with joy in her heart, that helped. They would spend their time having fun in the dwelling. Sometimes they would sing and dance. This grew their spirit stronger and gave them strength.

One day, they passed by their father. He looked up and seemed to have a moment of recognition. His eyes opened, and he reached out. Taken aback she walked over to him to hug him. Immersed in darkness immediately, she witnessed what he experienced. It remained a sad and dark place she saw and experienced through him. It affected her; she experienced where her Father remained in this darkness and it frightened and saddened her. Faith tried to pull her away. Drawn into her Father's darkness, his hands held onto her and would not let her go. Part of her wanted to stay, that was the trick of it, the darkness, it brought you into it, part of it made you believe you liked it and you wanted to be in it. The darkness remained evil and tricky. Those who might resist it must be very strong and very much of pure light. Her father tried to grab her harder and hug her, but this was not a hug and it was not love. Faith saw this. This was a new experience. She thought hard and remembered her tools. Faith realized if she grounded in her love for Hope it might help. Hope crumbled to the ground. Faith experienced panic. She would not lose her sister, and her assignment by her mother remained, to watch over her sister. He kept pulling, and Faith got a hold of Hope's arm and pulled and tugged, all the while sending love to Hope. Hope looked pale and lifeless. With one last huge tug, with a strength she didn't realize she possessed, she pulled Hope away from her Father. She kept pulling her away to distance them, dragging her sister out of desperation. She filled her heart with love for her sister. The strength and love for Hope prevailed. Faith broke Hope loose from her father's demonic grip. When they separated, she witnessed her Father's eyes and face with a grimace. He looked possessed. He made deep growling sounds. She tugged and dragged her sister along and away as fast as she could. It was very difficult, and all around were others filled with different stages of this darkness.

Somehow by an act of God or love, she got Hope to the door. The handle shone. Hope laid on the ground. Faith opened the door and rolled and pushed her inside. She experienced angst that a possibility existed that she would lose her sister. She stayed in that moment and held the love. Faith got a thick blanket right inside the door and laid it down and rolled her lifeless sister on the blanket. Her sister remained pale. She had a weak pulse. Faith gathered what she needed to help her sister. She got a cool cloth and held it in her hands for a few moments infusing it with love and life. Her mother had taught her how to do this and it served a purpose right now. She wished her mother stayed here but also recognized this continued to be a real learning moment and it remained important for her, to be alone in it and see if she might manage the whole event. At what cost though, what if she lost her sister? Faith continued to work on her, she wiped her sister's face and arms. Next she cleaned her scrapes from pulling her along the ground and dressed them. Then she rinsed a cloth in another solution which smelled of lavender. Faith put this on her sister's forehead and took her hand and felt her pulse again, no change. She accepted it would be a long night. She got up and scooped some warm broth into two bowls. One for her which she drank down to give her more strength. It remained important to take care of herself first, if it meant it would keep her strong. Then she would have more to give Hope. It would be an important lesson, sometimes the healer had to come first. Next she spooned little bits into her sister's mouth, tiny little spoons of the life-giving broth. Her sister made little gulps and choked a small amount of broth down. A hint of color and life returned to her face. Faith ran all the things she had learned like a checklist, making sure she took what she needed. After she got broth into her sister, she sat right by her crossed legged and laid her hands above her sister to infuse her with life giving energy, a technique her mother had taught her. Her mother and her had practiced this often in many situations, but never one matching this. It was a healing technique she hoped would help. She held her hands above the body and moved them from head to toe. She sensed Hope's energy; it seemed weak. As she worked her energy field, the body built in strength. She realized she shouldn't do too much when someone endured a weak state like this. After a short while, she stopped and then laid down next to her sister and fell asleep.

The next morning, when Faith awoke, she realized that her sister looked better, she still slept, so Faith got up and did chores. She made a new batch of brew, a different kind, to give to her sister when she woke up. Next she put special vegetable they had harvested in a magical place into the broth. She appreciated only to use this in extreme circumstances as it was a long trip to get more. This vegetable did not grow everywhere. Her sister moved restlessly for a while and then stilled. In the early afternoon, Hope opened her eyes and saw her sister staring at her with so much love. At that moment, there took place a real recognition they were sisters. She didn't understand how she knew, she just did, the connection, the twinship. Faith grinned as she recognized what Hope realized. Hope experienced weakness but sat up and her sister fed her the special broth and vegetables she had made. Hope became stronger, sensing the light within her grow. Faith understood it would take a while but her sister would recover. Hope rose and moved to the sitting area where they talked at length about what had happened.

Faith explained that she would continue to help Hope get strong and they would continue the exercises of going out. Faith would teach her much, and new ways to keep her strength up. She told Hope that she would know when she was ready to leave them and return to the village and Gracemama. Days passed, Hope got stronger in every way, and Faith was feeling better about how Hope was progressing. They both realized how important all this was. There were still pieces missing for Hope. Pieces of her past were missing, but they would come in time. Faith explained that it wasn't important right now.

One morning, they woke up, and there stood a woman in the kitchen cooking. She shone like a star. Her hair was black as night and cascaded down and below her waist. She looked present to what she cooked. Their mother had set the table. The table looked special and had the most beautiful, neon flowers in the center. One saw their life force. They looked like wildflowers. Hope just stared. Faith began moving and noticed that her mother worked in the kitchen. She smiled and looked at Hope with a nod. Then she said as if in reverence, "Yes this is our mother." They looked at her as she moved. She moved so gracefully, like floating on a cloud. Her feet bare, her skin polished tan by the sun and health exuded from her. She contained a lightness and energy about and around her. When she finished, she walked the food to the table. Mother gave the twins the gentlest loving smile. The girls sensed it; it touched them. Mother wore a piece of jewelry, Hope noticed it. It was a gold and silver heart of some sort that looked like it opened and contained something. The locket had holes in it and from within it sent a light out. The girls perceived a glow coming from inside. It caught Hope's attention, but just for a moment. Then her gaze returned to her mother's face. It was so peaceful and beautiful. Mother gave off life-force. Hope experienced it. She gave the girls a signal, and they got dressed so they could join her at the table. They understood what mother wanted without words.

Mother spoke after they ate their meal. Faith knew a lot of what she would say, so she directed the conversation towards Hope. "We have a purpose here, and we, Faith and I, must be here, that is a part of it. Your purpose Hope is to gain strength and knowledge at the village. At some point, we will meet you outside of the village and return together to get rid of this awful darkness. We will return as a Force like no one has ever seen. That is why you must go back and learn all you can and become strong, we need you for this undertaking. Faith and I must keep the light alive here so that the remaining people like us can stay strong. There are few like us, and we need everyone. We hope they can hold their light. Study hard with us for the short time you will be with us. The time is nearing when you will leave and go back to Gracemama."

"Gracemama and the women, their purpose is to work with you and teach you. They will take care of you and share in their knowledge. Each person you come into contact with there, that Gracemama puts you with will have something specific to teach you, they are a piece of the puzzle for you. You will become powerful. Don't let it scare you. It should not. This will take time and time is running out. We are not sure if we can hold the village from a complete takeover of the darkness. This has happened before to other villages far away, but they never had the ability to put out the darkness." Hope overwhelmed by hearing this, and a little frightened, didn't want to leave Faith and Mother ever again. She realized in her heart she must. Otherwise, this place and the people in it would die. This remained their purpose together. Hope decided at that moment to be strong, brave, and learn as much as she could. Mother read this on her face and smiled. She appreciated it was a lot for such a young girl, she also realized it must be. Hope was capable of this task. They ate breakfast after that. The food differed from what Faith had made. Even the aromas affected her. The food possessed a sweetness and contained love and nourishment in a way she had never felt. Her mother was a healer. This reflected in the food, and in many other ways Hope noticed. As they ate, each one was in their own thoughts.

One day, her mother took her in the room to the left of the dressing room. She had wondered what was in there. Mother taught her about healing with herbs and showed Hope how to use her hands for healing. They would leave the village and go out into the forests and fields around the village. She would teach her about everything growing in nature and the animals, rocks and stones. She taught her how to follow tracks of footprints of the animals. Her mother would show her how to survive in the wilderness, to find shelter and caves and water. She also taught her how to notice the plants that were poisonous and those that could fuel her as food. Sometimes Faith would join her, sometimes she had other duties to attend to. The women back at the camp would elaborate on what she was learning, but her mother started her off.

Another day, Mother and Hope came to a big field of wheat. They had traveled far and been out for a few days. It looked familiar. Jewelmama explained to her that this was the way back to the camp on foot. Hope took this route when she ran from their village to get to Gracemama. Hope remembered. This is the way she came to the camp of the women. Her instructions were to run as the darkness persisted in trying to stop her. With mother's help, she had gotten away from the darkening village, it was like she was superhuman. Mother had gotten her out of the village and left Faith to tend their home. Faith remained in their home alone until her mother returned. Even Faith had helped mother hold the energy as Hope traveled, by supporting Mother. Their mother returned to Faith once Hope was on her way. They held vigil the whole time, and because of Mother's gifts, she perceived where Hope was and propelled her on.

She must continue moving until she arrived at her destination. Mother hoped she would make it. Fortunately for all of them, she did. Mother had put her in a hypnotic state or trance for this feat. It was a rare thing to do but necessary if they had any chance of saving the village through Hope. She had been chosen to do this. This was part of her purpose. She ran day and night and was not even aware of it. She had told Hope before she left she would lose her memory for a while but she would regain it. That was happening; she remembered pieces. Faith was to stay back with mother. Distraught at first, because her sister, her twin sister, had to leave. They had always been inseparable. She had to help Mother with things there and to keep their home safe. The darkness outside their door grew. The door stayed closed during the time Faith's mother was away. Even the marker, the shiny door knob was not visible that day until her mother returned and touched it. Mother made everything sparkle and shine. Both had to recover for a while. They continued their work once they recovered, and Mother could see that Hope had made it. Mother also saw her collapse and the women take her away and knew the women would help her recover if possible. She knew this purpose was so strong for Hope that she couldn't let her feelings get in the way. Mother and Faith went about their business every day keeping as much light as they could. Hope was weak when she arrived; they knew she was coming. Jewelmama had communicated this with Gracemama, who was the wise woman at the camp. Gracemama was the most powerful, so Mother knew she was in the best of hands.

Hope had been with her mother and sister for what seemed a long time now. It was necessary. Now, Mother spoke to Hope and explained it is time for her to return. It was nighttime. Mother explained to Hope that when she awoke in the morning, she would be back in the camp.

She once again explained to Hope that she needed to listen and learn from Gracemama everything she could. Mother told her this might be awhile and not to worry about the time. She needed to be strong in her skills when she returned. That was the most important thing. If she wasn't, they wouldn't succeed. Hope drifted off to sleep after hugging her mother and her sister. She did not want to go back, but she understood she must.

CHAPTER FIVE
Learning Begins

Hope slept deeply and did not dream; her body rested. When she awoke, she opened her eyes. She remembered Mother's words, she would return to the camp. Slowly her vision focused on her surroundings. She spotted all the women around her holding the space for her return. Her heart warmed as she beheld the love and caring in their eyes. They were all present, Gracemama and the others. The women kept a vigil the whole time she was gone, taking shifts. They realized today she would return, so they all gathered yesterday to hold space for her safe return and change to being back with them again. She tried to move; it seemed as if her body clicked back into place. She sensed the change. It was different, not a familiar experience. After spending time with her mother and sister, she understood all of this more clearly. Her mother explained and taught her much while she was there. Hope rested with the women who stayed making sure she was all right. They kept healing energy around her and the group.

A few hours later, she indicated that she wanted to sit up. She spoke. Hope found it interesting that her voice came out, and they understood her. Something had taken place. One woman helped her sit. Another woman stepped out of the group and returned with a bowl of broth with vegetables in it. They gave her tea, always tea. She liked the food with all the flavors. Even the steam rising gave off wonderful aromas. She ate and drank and became restored. Her energy returned. She smiled, and they realized a change had occurred. They perceived no fear in Hope's eyes.

The fact intrigued Hope at the way she left and returned like this. She experienced emotions toward missing her sister and Mother but recognized and accepted her mission. Gracemama could detect the resolve in the girl's eyes. Hope looked forward to a time when she would see her family again. She now knew she was here to learn to help her village. The group broke up after hugging her and left. Gracemama stayed with Hope. The girl stood up just to walk around the hut. She sensed her body. She now seemed to have an increased sensitivity to her surroundings. Gracemama nodded in understanding. She had wisdom and experienced much in her life. This was not the time to talk about her past; this was the time to care for and teach Hope. She was literally "The Hope" for the future. She had the potential to become wise and powerful if she immersed herself in learning. Gracemama would be sure she would be taught in the correct way, all the while being nurtured with love. That is why Mother had sent her here. Gracemama gave her a few days to acclimate and then her learning would begin. This would be a serious undertaking. Everyone had returned to the camp. She would meet more of the women and become familiar with her surroundings. They would go to the caves for more intense teaching later.

The sun had gone down, and Gracemama got her sleeping area prepared. Hope followed suit as she looked at Gracemama she mimicked her. She was there to learn and thought she would show she understood that. She wanted to show deep respect to Gracemama. The women had accepted her into their place with love. After they lay down, Gracemama spoke. She said, "I will say a prayer and my goodnight blessings. Listen, because I will teach them to you soon." Hope listened to the sweet words of prayer and a little melody. She understood the words. She wanted to learn the prayers. Hope realized she must learn all she could to help her mother and sister save the village. After the prayer, Hope said sweetly, "Thank you and good night." Gracemama smiled, it warmed her heart.

In the early morning Hope perceived the slightest hint of light coming through a crack in the doorway curtain. She laid in her spot thinking about everything that already transpired. Hope welcomed learning and this new challenge. Her youth contributed to her missing her mother and sister more. Hope appreciated the kindness, love and care the women showed her.

She got up and moved around. Hope realized Gracemama was not in sight. This was the first time alone. She liked the peace and safety this hut brought her, and she didn't mind being alone here. Hope sat up and surveyed the room. She recognized steam coming from the cooking pot. Gracemama or someone had left her food. She heard her tummy rumbling as the aroma drifted her way. After a while, she walked over and caught sight of an empty bowl and cup sitting on the table. Hope scooped the porridge up into the bowl and filled the cup with drink and sat down to eat. The food gave her strength. After eating, she changed her clothes. A set of clothes lay at the bottom of her sleeping area. Hope slipped into them, tied a string neckline that made a simple bow and then put on the moccasin type shoes which had fringe. She ran her hands over the soft fabric. She wiggled her toes in the comfortable foot coverings. Hope found the clothes practical, easy to move in, yet pretty. She noticed a little leather bag she felt inclined to put on. She looked inside it first. In the bag she found herbs and a few small stones. For now, she put it on. She would ask Gracemama about it. She discovered a hair tie and pulled her long black hair into a low ponytail to have it out of her face. A bowl of water and cloth sat nearby which she used to wash her face. Then she found fresh mint leaves which she rubbed her teeth with. She had seen Gracemama do this.

Hope noticed movement and low talking outside of the hut. Between her curiosity and the need to relieve herself she decided to go outside. She walked toward the doorway and pushed the curtain aside. A woman sat by the door on a stump working with a carving knife making a bowl. The woman looked at the girl and smiled. She said she waited there for Hope to show her around. Her name was Clove. Hope had met her before. She was the flute lady. Clove knew the girl would need to relieve herself. She motioned to Hope as she stood up, and told her she would show her a place to take care of her needs, to relieve herself. Hope understood her when she talked and spoke back acknowledging this. They walked to the edge of the camp.

They walked on a narrow trail single file. Hope looked around so she could get her bearings and find this place again. She noticed many people milling around the camp. Everyone seemed to have a task or was headed somewhere. Hope followed Clove to a small closet type building. Clove opened the door, inside she saw a seat with a hole. On the floor was a bag of something and some fresh leaves nearby in a pile. Clove explained to use the leaves for cleaning after taking care of her personal needs. They looked soft. The bag contained something that kept everything down the hole dissolving. Its name is lime, which comes from limestone. It also helps with odor. Clove explained she should take one scoop and put it down the hole. It would dissolve the excrements. Hope sat down and did as explained after Clove shut the door. As she sat there, she looked up and around and saw several fresh bouquets of herbs hanging from the ceiling. The sweet smell in this place was unexpected. When finished, she exited. Clove waited for her a little way down the trail. They headed back to the village. This place was within the perimeter but off and away from the huts. Clove walked at a nice pace; it seemed like they were heading somewhere. They headed to a big hut in a central location. Clove headed to a door on the side and let Hope know she would be outside waiting. Hope entered.

Gracemama waited for her inside. Many things hung on the shelves. Hope saw bowls, cookware, and utensils. In another part of the room, she identified musical instruments on shelves. There were sitting places around a long table and a few more tables scattered about. Hope saw a work area to cook against one wall. The work area appeared to be long, and she guessed several people could be there at once.

Gracemama sat in a chair off to the corner. She showed Hope to sit in the chair next to her. She had two cups of tea which they drank together. Next, Gracemama explained to her that learning would begin here and on this day. Hope was ready. Gracemama had more to say. She told Hope that she would learn about the healing abilities of all the plants in this room. She would teach her much, and each plant had much to teach. They walked around the room and tables. Gracemama talked about the many types of hanging plants. As she did, she named them. She did not expect Hope to remember all this, but she had to start somewhere to familiarize her with the information. She showed her the mortar and pestle to crush the plant's leaves, and other tools they would use, she explained the plants hung to dry. There is a way to use the plants when alive and fresh, and with her gift, the plants might even speak to her, teach her. Hope did not understand this, but that was not important right now. Today's purpose was so that Hope would become familiar with this gathering and eating place.

It had been a long day and Hope's head swam. Gracemama ended with more talking and a prayer to close the day. She told Hope that Clove waited for her outside. She would take her back to their hut and she could rest. Gracemama said she would see her later at dinner. She had things to attend to. She seemed old and wise, but Hope wondered how and where she got all this energy. Hope departed out of the door and left Gracemama sitting in her chair with a smile. Clove sat outside the door. She rose, and they headed toward the hut. The sunshine warmed her. The day happened to be a bright and sunny day, so people walked around going about their business. Hope got curious about all the others. Being more disciplined, she headed to the hut. She realized she needed to take a break and rest. She lay down. Clove covered her with a blanket. Hope quickly drifted off to sleep. She did not hear Clove say, "I will be back for you later." Hope slept soundly with no dreams.

Hope sensed a hand on her forehead stroking her hair back. Then a gentle hand on her shoulder to wake her up. She opened her eyes to see Clove sitting there. They stayed this way for a while. Hope adjusted to her surroundings in the present moment. She took her time then sat up on her sleeping place. She looked across the room and detected a bowl of food and a drink for her. Her tummy rumbled again. This learning made her hungry, she chuckled to herself. She walked over and sat down to eat. There would be a full meal soon so the bowl did not contain a lot of food. After eating she walked over to the pitcher and bowl and washed her face. This time after she poured warm water into the bowl, an aroma rose up. What was that familiar aroma? She had perceived the scent earlier in the learning room. Hope remembered, the aroma was lavender. She dipped the cloth in it and washed her face. A comb lay next to the bowl. She used it to redo her hair after resting. She saw a fresh long dress; Clove told her to change into it. The dress looked pretty and had stitching on it. It fell just below her knees. She put her moccasins on. The rest and food renewed her. Clove had watched her through her process. She understood what to do. She seemed to be learning the routines. It would provide normalcy while she was here.

Clove realized her responsibility toward the girl was immense. Gracemama gave her the honor to look after Hope and explained some reasons Hope was here. She knew this girl had been given a huge responsibility. Clove became Hope's watcher and keeper when she was not with Gracemama and took this seriously. Clove maintained a very warm heart toward Hope. She could sense this wonderful spirit in the girl and would give her one-hundred percent. She remembered the experience of learning and training as she had gone through it. Clove possessed her own gifts. Sometimes it was overwhelming, a lot to learn, and scary, but Hope must walk this path to hone her skills. Every person had gifts and every person's gifts were unique. That was the beauty of it. Gracemama possessed the gift of seeing what each person possessed that made them a unique, individual and nurturing it. Gracemama surpassed all the others in age and wisdom. She knew about the history of the surrounding places. She would be tough if necessary and would let each individual go through the tests they must when they studied with her. Clove thought of all the teaching she had received from Gracemama. She was thankful for it now.

It was time for Hope to go out into the village and be around other people. She would expand from the group of seven and Gracemama. Clove indicated that they were going out. Hope was rested and in a good state to receive and meet others. They walked out into the sunlight. It was bright on their eyes, and they squinted. Clove took Hope's hand to lead her back to the gathering and eating hut. When they entered, she saw the long table all set up for eating. Around it were many people. Around the rest of the room, other long tables were set up that hadn't been there filled with more people. Somehow the whole village had gathered here. Everyone was silent when Hope entered. She was led to the table to sit down. Clove sat down next to Hope. They appreciated the purpose in this gathering was to welcome and meet Hope. As Hope sat, Gracemama stood. She clapped her hands three times. Hope had heard her do this before as a signal that something significant was about to happen. Everyone turned to Gracemama, and she spoke. First she said a blessing over the people and the food, then over Hope. Next she stated that they would break bread together. Then they ate a delicious meal. It would keep their energy up. It would be a long evening.

Gracemama explained to them that Hope was to become one with all and be part of their village. Her purpose here was to learn much and as quickly as possible. She had a lot to learn and would need the support of everyone. Gracemama said a part of the group would help in Hope's teaching. Others would get various tasks to assist her in other ways. Sitting around the table were the other women from the camp. She had seen them around the village that day. After the meal and her talk, Gracemama got up and led Hope to every person in the room. Gracemama introduced each person, gave their name, a little about each one and their specific specialty. As they experienced this process, it almost seemed like Gracemama was melding the energy between Hope and the person she was meeting. At the end, she felt part of the whole. They walked back to their seats.

A small group of women stepped onto a raised wooden platform, like a stage, and sang. It was ethereal. The women possessed the most beautiful voices. It was

49

hypnotic. One pulled out a drum, another a flute, another a gourd which contained seeds that would rattle, and a few instruments she didn't recognize. It was a language which spoke to her heart. It made her experience lots of emotions and love. These women shared a deep part of themselves. They gave to her, it was their gift to her. One by one after a while each person got up. The structure was huge and there was an area that was empty. They left their chairs and danced to the rhythm. It was beautiful to watch. There was a basket on the side, and some would take out a colorful piece of cloth or a small instrument, and they all became one in sound and movement, vibration and color. After a while Gracemama and Clove took Hope to the center, and they danced. Clove showed Hope a simple step which Hope would develop into her own dance. She joined in slowly at first, the music sped up, and the dance did too. It was freeing, healing, and joyful. It was the universal language, and she could sense the vibration throughout her body. They danced for a long time. Hope smiled and laughed a lot on this day. The purpose was to welcome Hope in this celebration. The celebration ran late into the evening. Exhausted, Gracemama, Hope, and Clove walked back to the hut. They drank tea. Clove left, and they slept. The camp was quiet.

In the morning, different from other days, everyone slept late. This day would be different. She would tour the village so she would appreciate it as her own. The purpose of this day happened to be for the people to meet and get to know Hope better. In the evening, they all met in the large structure to eat their meal together and close the ceremony. Tomorrow, Clove explained that everyone would go back to their daily life. She told Hope she would be with her sometimes, but she would spend time with Gracemama learning also, alone just the two of them. Hope would be on her own sometimes. Clove prepared tea for them so that Hope would sleep deeply. While she slept, she would dream and learn. Not every night, but sometimes.

CHAPTER SIX

Getting Lost

Hope awoke refreshed. Her senses seemed heightened. She beheld every little sight and sound. She looked around the room. No one was there; she was alone. She spotted food and drink on the table. Hope liked the quiet and being alone. She felt safe in the hut. She ate and then washed up and dressed for the day. There were clothes neatly folded by the changing and washing area. Hope recognized the path to the outbuilding where she wanted to go. She walked there, once she finished, she followed the method shown to her and put a scoop of the mixture down the hole. Hope looked up and spotted a fresh bouquet hanging from the ceiling creating a sweet aroma. She left the outhouse and stood outside the door looking at her surroundings. Hope saw no one was around.

She walked a short distance on the path. She discovered many sounds. Hope detected the tiniest of animals hopping around or crawling through the brush. Hope experienced heightened senses. The birds sang in full chorus. She heard the crunching of dry leaves as little creatures moved about unseen. It seemed peaceful here in this wooded area. As she wandered, she stepped off the path to pick the most beautiful flower, then another and another. She spotted more flowers. She did this for quite a while. When she looked up, she didn't recognize where she was. Her stomach tightened. Hope became frightened as she held this beautiful bouquet. Turning around three-hundred-sixty-degrees, she recognized nothing and realized she should not have stepped off the path.

Hope remembered an old trick her mother taught her. As she walked around, she tried to find a familiar spot and she dropped the flowers as a marker from where she'd been. She made a trail so she would find her way back to at least where she started. Hope walked for a long time; her bouquet was down to a few flowers. The air cooled off, and the light decreased. The noises she heard persisted and were not so friendly anymore. Hope sat down and cried. She became tired and hungry but she didn't want to fall asleep in this unfriendly spot. Something about this spot made her more tired. The darkness she experienced in her village visiting her mother and sister seemed similar. The girl tried to think and remember what she could do. Hope learned from her mother to focus on her and Hope's sister when she wanted to call upon them. She recognized they would identify what to do. Hope felt frightened.

Hope understood from her sister they possessed a permanent bond of connection through thought. She remembered that. Hope sat down on the spot she tried to relax. She remembered she needed to be in a relaxed state, and to receive love and think of her mom and sister.

She did just that, and the intensity grew and expanded. Gradually, after what seemed a long time, she saw an image of her mother and sister in her mind's eye. They stood side by side glowing with light. Hope held this vision while she also emanated a glow. She sensed great love in seeing them. She heard her mom say, "Remember the answers are within you. You realize what to do." Hope relaxed and continued the exercise. She thought about what to do to get back to where she came from. Her mom and sister continued to be with her in her mind's eye supporting her.

Hope stood up, she didn't feel so alone and scared anymore. She followed the flower trail she had laid down. She continued to emanate light as the darkness receded. When she got to where the flowers ended, a short distance away, she saw the path. Hope realized that she did not wander far off, her fear made her panic. If she remained grounded and centered in herself, she might have realized that. She got back to the narrow little trail. She stood, closed her eyes, and experienced great love. Her mom nodded at her, and her sister smiled. They still sent her love, and she received it. Then she whispered, "I love you too." In the next moment, they disappeared. The sunlight receded as Hope headed back to the village. The girl knew where she was going now. Hope learned an important lesson today, she would not let this happen again. Be mindful, know your surroundings, and stay grounded and centered always. Keep the love around, and that will help with protection. Darkness doesn't like love and light. As she walked back, she found herself different, and that she had changed just ever so slightly from this experience. She noticed her body in movement and experienced the ground under her feet. A tiny glow surrounded her, which was not there before. She did not see this, but it became the first little step toward her inner light and power growing within her. One of her first lessons. She got back to the hut. People milled around. She headed straight in. No one was there. She was tired, and so she laid down and slept a good deep sleep. While she slept, she integrated this new experience into her cells, her mind, and the rest of her body.

Hope awoke, she was still alone. She sat up cross legged on her bedding, with a straight back and hands on knees. It seemed good, aligned. She took a deep breath, this too was agreeable. She closed her eyes and sat quietly in deep thought. Hope reviewed the events she experienced. She understood she needed to keep the light about her and she realized that love was the key. She thought about the food she consumed since she got here and how it was so life-giving. The teas she drank always seemed to be made with a purpose, to relax, be alert, and she was sure there was a purpose to many of the things that Gracemama and the other women did. Hope already learned something just by being here. She rose and walked to where Gracemama taught her how to use different plants for various teas. The girl always looked at how she brewed the teas. She learned one tea that made one alert, another good for a tummy ache or headache, and some other properties of various teas. Hope took the tiniest bit of one she remembered as good for her tummy. It also helped one to be alert. This dried tea was potent. She made some hot water by using the hot fire embers; she added some nearby tinder to get the flames reignited, then some larger pieces of wood and brewed herself some tea. Hope walked over to an already made pot of broth and vegetables and served herself a bowl. She ate it with reverence as she recognized the life force food could have on one's energy. She ate deliberately trying to notice the flavors and different vegetables. Hope realized she had accomplished some new tasks on her own today which made her proud.

Hope cleaned up, washed her face and walked outside. People milled around and some said hello. She greeted them back with a smile. Clove had shown her where she stayed, a few huts down. She walked there and called her name at the door. Clove came out. Hope asked about Gracemama. Clove explained she had to go somewhere and did not know when she would return. She told Hope if she needed anything she could help her. Hope said she would be fine. Clove nodded and walked back into her home. What Clove didn't tell Hope is that Gracemama told her to leave Hope alone unless she asked for help until she got back. Gracemama wanted her to have time, and she understood she would learn lessons. She needed to become more independent. Clove should be there to assist if needed, but otherwise, left by herself. Hope wandered over to the big gathering hut.. She then walked to the area where Gracemama had been teaching her. She stayed quite a while reviewing the plants and herbs and what she had learned. It was sinking in. After studying the plants, she left the building and wandered the village. People proceeded with their daily chores, walking somewhere or conversing with others. She started recognizing the faces of everyone. People would greet her as she walked around. She stopped and talked with a few, just being friendly. The conversations not too long, just enough to show her interest in the others. She wandered the outer ring of the huts. She now moved to the inner ring where she knew the women better. They were special and there for anything she might need. She passed by Clove's hut again, she saw her sitting out on a stump carving what looked like a bowl. It had beautiful carvings on it. There appeared to be a second uncarved piece of wood in a longer shape. Clove looked up and greeted Hope. Clove asked Hope if she needed anything or if she would like to sit with her. Hope took the second stump and sat down. She watched Clove intently. Her work seemed intricate. The bowl appeared to be especially beautiful. The color a brownish reddish type of wood with lines of the grain showing. They talked a little. Clove moved inside and brought Hope a cup of tea. The drink tasted sweet and relaxed her. She told Clove she might see her later and returned to her hut. Hope was tired. She did not see Gracemama so she laid down on her bed and fell asleep.

When she awoke, Gracemama startled her. She sat near her looking at her; she had returned sooner than she had planned. Hope calmed down. Gracemama stroked her forehead. After a while Gracemama got up and went to the table they ate at. Food sat on the table. She indicated for Hope to come over so they might eat and talk. Hope rose slowly, she had been in a deep sleep. The aroma from the food made her hungry. Some bread with seeds in it and nut butter sat on the table. She followed Gracemama's lead and spread it on her bread and took a bite. It was delicious. After they finished, the time came for Gracemama to speak to Hope. She had things to explain to her. They needed to increase Hope's learning. Gracemama explained there were places they needed to go. There were activities they needed to do together, and some activities for Hope to do alone. She needed to test her skills after she learned more. Now they would travel to the caves, a special place for learning. Gracemama would go to the caves for various reasons, one of which was to build up her strength and stamina.

They then discussed what happened when Hope got lost. Hope was totally befuddled how Gracemama knew about it. She had knowledge of every detail. She told Hope she had to always be aware and mindful of her surroundings or something could happen. Gracemama said she came close to danger, and she wasn't sure if Hope could have saved herself. This was why they must get going on her learning. She told Hope it was smart to leave the trail of flowers. Once Hope slowed down and stopped being as afraid, she did the correct things. She knew she had connected with her mother and sister and said that was one of the most important skills she could learn and use because they would always be there to assist her. That connection was strong, but Hope had to remember to connect, and when fear gets in your way, you don't always remember the practical steps. She agreed that Hope needed to practice being grounded. Grounded meant being connected to the earth through her feet, solid, and present to what was going on around her. Gracemama also explained the success of the whole experience. Getting out of her predicament and back on the path was an important lesson. It had built the strength of her inner light just a little, but that was what her goal needed to be to have a very powerful light within. That was what would help her. It was what would chase the darkness away. This was one of the most important skills Hope needed when the time came to saving her village. She needed to become strong in this ability.

"Enough talk," said Gracemama. It was late now, and they had talked a lot. Hope had questions. Gracemama answered every one of them. Gracemama told Hope it was time to sleep and get rest as tomorrow morning they would leave the village for the caves at early light. She had already talked to the other women of their little group so they understood what was happening and would come if needed. They would venture out to the surrounding areas. Hope would learn a great deal during this trip. She had the ability, there would be moments it would test her to her limit. In the past, Hope would have experienced fear by all this responsibility. She was young. But she understood this was the only way to help her mother and sister and the village. She decided for bravery, courage, and willingness to do anything for that goal. Hope had a wisdom far beyond her young years. She had not realized that wisdom yet. Hope lay down and thought about all the events coming up and that had happened. She drifted into a deep sleep. The women in the group would sleep when they could because they were on call if needed during this time while Hope and Gracemama went to the caves.

CHAPTER SEVEN

Resettlement

At morning light Gracemama gently woke Hope up. They ate a quick breakfast and practiced their morning routine. A pack stood by Hope's bed that contained everything she would need. The women prepared it the day before. Last, the girl put on her walking shoes and both Gracemama and Hope, with their personal packs on their backs, headed out through the door. They left the village at a quick pace. Gracemama could walk at a fast pace, this surprised Hope. She knew this trip would take all day and wanted to get going. In the past, Gracemama made this trip many times. It seemed they walked for hours on the trail which, in time, opened into a big field.

The trail stopped. Gracemama explained that the reason for this was so that no one could follow the trail to the caves. She showed Hope how the field looked circular, and had a north, south, east, and west. They came in on the South side. Now they faced north and would travel in that direction. Trees and forest surrounded the field except in one area off between the North and the West portions. As they stood there, Gracemama talked to Hope. She pointed to the opening in the tree line and explained to Hope they would walk in that direction. She then told Hope to turn around and look to where they were standing. Hope saw that the spot in the exact south where they stood contained the same features and opening, no trees tightly growing together. Off the path, just a step from where they stood in the trees were rocks hidden at the base of a tree. These rocks formed a circle with a few missing on the entrances and exit. There was also one on the other side like this that Gracemama would show her. These rocks were not ordinary rocks, they were firmly in the ground and of a different shape. The rocks appeared carved with design. Gracemama pulled out a necklace that she wore around her neck and inside her clothing. Hope saw a large pendant, circular and plain. It did not seem like much. Gracemama opened it, Hope gasped, it was beautiful inside. That was the trick, the inside. It had beautiful designs on the disc; it too represented where they had traveled to and from with a few tiny jewels in it to indicate important spots. No one would realize this was a map, a small tiny representation of where they were traveling with important trail markings.

Gracemama explained the map and the markings in great detail after they spread out a cloth on the ground and had a meal. She took food out of her pack which they ate. Gracemama said they should lie down for a short rest as they would walk all afternoon. It would rejuvenate them. Sleeping was as important as time spent awake. Gracemama woke Hope up after a while with a gentle shake. Hope came around and recognized the sun had shifted. Gracemama was teaching her to notice these things. Hope helped Gracemama pack up everything, then they left on their way across the field. It was a beautiful day for traveling. They reached the other side of the field and entered where Gracemama had shown Hope they would. As they walked, they noticed stones like the other ones. A new wider trail began here as they entered the deep thick forest. They walked on this trail for about an hour and then came out of the woods. Soon after the trail narrowed, the terrain changed. The path sloped upward, scattered around the landscape appeared rocks, plants and trees. The weather remained agreeable as they continued on. About an hour into this part of the walk, they stopped and left the path. Again a marker marked this spot where they walked off the trail. They came to a small clearing with a place that had a fire pit. Most of the time they made their own fire. This time Gracemama gave instructions to others to have this stop ready to go. The fire was ready and just needed to be lit. Gracemama left for a moment and came back with a jug of water, a pot to heat it, and a sealed container with tea. They took about an hour break between starting the fire, making their drink, and eating a small amount of food from Gracemama's pack. When they finished their meal, they returned everything back to where it belonged and used the remaining water to douse the fire. To extinguish any remaining embers, Gracemama instructed Hope to cover the spot with dirt. They walked back to the trail and continued. Now mid afternoon they noticed the incline became steeper. Big boulders appeared in their path, some of which they had to climb over. The two of them managed, and after some time the walk evened out. They had several ways to get to the caves. Gracemama picked the one most traveled. They were on a ridge which they followed. They could see over both sides, and it was expansive. After traveling for a while they came to a spot where the terrain changed and they descended. The ground became more level again, and they followed the path. The terrain had various grasses with different textures, rocks, and trees.

CHAPTER EIGHT

The Caves

Early evening descended upon them. They entered a different area where Hope noticed a sheer rock wall to the right. They followed this wall. As they turned they passed through some thick tree growth which opened up suddenly. Hope heard water running off in the distance as they followed the rock wall. This area appeared hidden with growth and trees on the perimeter. They stopped for a moment and Hope looked up and down and all around. What was this place? It seemed special, almost cocoon like. Trees appeared on the top of the wall that grew sideways like a roof or overhang. During the whole trip Gracemama knew where they were going. This became clear when she led them to this hidden place. Hope spotted an opening in the wall about five feet high and five feet wide. They stepped into it. What Hope saw didn't look like anything from the outside and trees blocked the view to the entrance. When they stepped in, Hope's jaw dropped. She would not have imagined this secret room. The room glowed with a fire burning in a pit in the center of the room. The room had a warmth and coziness and the walls glowed a warm brownish orange.

This room was large and contained a sleeping area, a cooking and eating area. Another area looked like a workshop with containers filled with various items. Plants hung from the ceiling drying, as well as stones, crystals, and many other items. Hope viewed a sitting place and two sleeping areas. The room appeared neat and tidy, taken care of and readied for their arrival. Gracemama often liked to come here. The wise woman would come here to her special place to rejuvenate, learn, and go inward.

At the table a meal waited for them with steam rising off the cooked food. Gracemama showed Hope her sleeping area; fresh clothes sat on her bed folded. A washbowl stood on a stand of her own and contained warm water. She looked at the steam rising. She walked over to the washbowl to clean up from the long journey. A screen provided an area to give her privacy when she washed and dressed. She changed and moved over to the table. Before they ate, Gracemama said blessings out loud, the ones Hope remembered, so she joined in. They ate their meal and Hope delighted in all the flavors once again. A sound or two escaped her. She ate and drank till she filled up her tummy with food; next she rubbed her belly to show how full she had become. Hope yawned as the day concluded. She walked over to her bed and went to sleep.

Refreshed from sleeping, the two got up and proceeded through the morning routine. They took time to settle in. After a while, Gracemama pointed to the sitting area. In this area Hope spotted some very comfortable seating. The chairs seemed perfect for their bodies. The girl sank into hers. Hope thought these were comfortable yet supportive, not chairs one would doze off in. Gracemama sat in her chair and pulled a little table in close. A bound book sat on the table, the book appeared thick and looked heavy.

Gracemama said a prayer again, this one over the book. The book had a latch for a key. The wise woman unlocked it with the special key which she retrieved from a hidden container. Before opening it, Gracemama explained most of what Hope had to learn would be in this book, and it was sacred and extremely special. Hope was to treat the book with great care and keep it in a special place when not being used. Created a long time ago, this book held much knowledge about many subjects. She explained that she would introduce the book to Hope and that the book had life to it and would get to know her. She asked Hope to be silent and place her hand on top of the book before they opened it. Hope did as the wise woman told her to and had the most interesting experience. It was as if the book loved her and was saying hello. She couldn't explain it any better than that. Her hand grew warm, and she felt like the book was getting to know all the intricacies of her palm. It seemed like a clear light of energy under her hand that traced her hand and all the lines on it. Then Gracemama smiled and told Hope to open it. What she saw inside was incredible. The beginning pages had these beautiful drawings of plants and flowers with writing next to them containing detailed explanations. It gave great detail of how to use them and everything one could do with each plant. Extremely smart and advanced, Hope had learned to read well at a young age. The words appeared in a different language but seemed to translate and change before Hope's eyes so she could understand them. The colors used on the drawings looked so real and vibrant. Hope understood that this book was a living thing. She could see it and sense it. She continued to turn the pages carefully. The book fascinated the girl; it contained so many subjects not just limited to plants or rocks or crystals. She found fascination in looking at the book for a while and getting to understand what it contained. The book and Gracemama would teach her. There were times the book would help her learn and infuse her with the knowledge. After a long while, Gracemama told her she should shut the book and lock it. They said a blessing and then returned the book and key to a safe place. She would study the book throughout their stay here. Gracemama told her to reference it whenever she wanted, and to treat the book with great respect. Tired the girl needed to absorb all this and sleep. They had spent most of the day working with the book. Tomorrow her learning and studies would continue.

Hope retired to her bed and slept. She had some dreams of what she had seen in the book. They were pleasant. The information was integrating itself into Hope's mind. She awoke rested. Gracemama was busy over where all the plants and herbs were. She was making something for Hope to drink later. Hope went about her business getting ready for the day. Even though she was in a different location, she recognized what Gracemama expected of her by now. There was a system to what they did. She would show Gracemama what she had learned.

She worked at using and putting it into practice. These tasks were easy, and it showed Gracemama independence. She stood a little taller today like she had grown up a little more just overnight. Hope felt peaceful and was ready to move forward. Together they discussed her backpack and what should be in it for travel. Different things would be packed for a day outing or a longer one. There were certain items she should always have in her pack. She didn't understand the use of some things but had confidence she would learn. It was time for breakfast. Hope and Gracemama had a quiet meal. Gracemama spoke to Hope to make her aware that they would go on a short day trip today to learn more about the plants and their different uses. Hope would then learn how to gather them and use them when needed.

CHAPTER NINE
Gaining Knowledge

After their meal, they threw their backpacks on in a hurry. Hope remained surprised at how spry Gracemama was at her age. They walked at a brisk pace for a while then slowed down. When the two of them left the cave area, they walked through a field and later into an area with some trees and a brook. They wandered this general area for several hours.

She showed Hope where things grew, helped Hope learn to identify them, and then they picked plants to take back to the cave. Gracemama taught her about foods she could eat and herbs to cook with. She explained to Hope what to use to heal and make teas with. She described how the wild plants had healing properties. One plant she had an interest in because of its wide spectrum of properties was lavender; it showed a beautiful little lavender flower now. Gracemama told the girl sage's purpose was to burn and clear area spaces and it had other properties. A food called watercress grew down by and into the bank of the brook. Used raw, its flavor is a little sharp and bitter. Watercress provided a nice taste to give a little kick to the food. It grew wild all along the bank and grew little round green leaves. They headed back to the caves after working all day. The items they gathered hung from their packs. They bound the stems of the plants with twine. They would hang to dry in the cave. Gracemama and Hope looked funny with these things hanging from their packs. The packs had lots of loops down the sides just for a purpose like this.

As the days progressed, Gracemama and Hope continued to go back out into the land beyond the caves. Some days they would venture out into different terrains. They would go for an overnight from time to time. The repetition helped Hope learn better, and she became good at recognizing the plants in the wild, and what to do with them when she got them back to the cave. She also learned on the overnights how to set up camp. Hope learned quickly for being so young.

Gracemama taught her to gather food, and also explained that when out in the wild sometimes she would need endurance. Physically they were strong from all their activity. She explained the food they ate could be helpful, such as fish, birds or meat from various other animals. During their time hunting animals, they hiked further away from the caves. They would go to a shelter hidden in the woods off any hiking trail and find them stocked with supplies. Buried in the ground they found tools and bows and arrows to hunt with.

Gracemama taught her the spiritual ritual of hunting and praying and thanking the animals for their lives. She first taught Hope to catch fish with her hands, then after to spear or lure them with a fishing line. Next, she taught her how to get birds on the ground and in a tree with a bow and arrow or a slingshot for small birds. For now, that was enough. Gracemama thought about if she needed to teach Hope to hunt larger animals. She decided, if so, that would come later. She would talk to her about it, and tell her what to do in case, but for now, there wasn't a need. Hope did not like killing animals and fish, but she knew it might come in handy. She was a gentle soul and much preferred eating of plant-based foods.

Gracemama and Hope spent many weeks at the cave implementing the use of all she had learned. Repetition seemed to be the key, and it was working. She learned what to do with everything, each item's purpose, and how to give thanks for the use of all that nature offered. It felt as if they were alone. In reality, there were people around taking care of them but they stayed out of their way.

This was a special place to learn. It would help to increase someone's knowledge at a faster pace because of the energy around. That is why they were here and Hope learned much in this stretch of time.

One night, Gracemama sat Hope down and told her it was time for them to have a serious talk. She told Hope that she had learned well and it was time to test that knowledge. Hope had left her village quite a while ago. She had sprouted like a weed in height and added weight to her frame. Hope had matured. Gracemama explained they would work in the coming days with growing her light and then she would go on a journey alone to test herself. Gracemama wanted to make sure Hope was up to the task. She would teach her how to navigate to get where she needed to go by reading the sun and the stars

71

and any other skills she might need for her journey. She would help Hope deepen her knowledge from the base of what she had already learned. The eventual goal was the bigger journey when she went back to her mother and sister.

They reviewed everything. Gracemama gave Hope some small tests. The wise woman reminded her of eating protein. Flesh of an animal or a fish became necessary because they needed the protein and the strength it had to give. Gracemama taught Hope to tan the hides of animals to make certain clothes, tools, and other things. The Wise One taught the girl to express reverence in using an animal or plant or anything where life ended. It was a great gift and sacrifice of that living plant, animal or fish. Hope understood this.

There was one last thing that Hope needed to learn. It was one of the most difficult things to learn but could save one's life. Gracemama said they would spend time with this and then Hope would go on her solo journey, her test to see if she was ready to go home again.

CHAPTER TEN

Touchstone and Invisibility

One morning very early after a good night's sleep, Gracemama woke up Hope and told her to get ready. They both took day packs. Overnight packs weighed more. They didn't travel too far from the caves. They entered a cleared area with a sparkling creek, lots of birds and butterflies. The place seemed magical, it made one happy to be there. Preparation took place before Hope arrived for this last learning. It contained all the things Gracemama understood Hope loved and made her heart sing. In the center of the clearing Hope beheld pure white fluffy animal skins. They were beautiful. When they sat down, cushioning was underneath. One received the beautiful sounds of nature. Gracemama explained to Hope that this spot was special and contained a touchstone for Hope to come back to in her mind and heart. This place would provide the setting needed. This was the last and most important time.

They ate fruit and nuts and drank tea prior to leaving this morning. Gracemama wanted their stomachs to be light, not full and heavy with food. Gracemama told Hope to relax and close her eyes, and Gracemama did the same. They sat and listened to the sounds of nature. After a while, Hope discovered the sweetest melody. A flute played, the sound sweet like honey. The sound resonated with her soul. She experienced the love and beauty. Another flute and another until there took place a gentle, sweet loving symphony of flutes. Gradually, she opened her eyes when Gracemama touched her knee. Around her, surrounding them at the outer edge of the clearing many women played these flutes. Butterflies and birds flew about. The place seemed to shimmer and transform. Gracemama instructed Hope to receive the beauty and the love and immerse herself into it. She did as instructed. As she did this, she seemed lighter. Hope sensed a happiness like none she had ever known, and a love, a deeper love. She bathed her mind and soul in it as she let go. As Hope did this, her physical body lightened and shimmered. She became a little transparent and then progressively more. She sat in the same spot, but no one could see her. The girl achieved invisibility. She perceived the love and beauty that filled her. Hope needed this impression and must remember it. She would never forget this experience. Gracemama taught her how to become invisible. They did this until Gracemama knew she had surrendered, and this state of being became clear and that she could return to it. The flutes stopped playing one by one. Birds and butterflies lessened. The last flute lowered its notes. Hope gradually returned to how she appeared in everyday life. She seemed heavier; she sensed love and beauty but not the way she had before. The flute played a low melody. From the woods, there came a sound, the low beat of a drum, it became louder and was a deep and earthly sound. The effect was undeniable; it brought one back to the moment. The music continued for a while before finally stopping. Hope seemed present and solid and sensed her body, she was not invisible any longer What happened here? She tried to understand it with her logical mind, which is not the way this worked. Hope experienced the contrast, the lightness she experienced and later moving into her body and the solid quality it brought back. Both states were important to know. Hope would see the sense of it later.

After they took a rest on the blankets, Gracemama explained. The music was her song, Hope's song, created for her. Gracemama explained what happened, she learned to become invisible. She experienced a higher vibration to the point of invisibility. There was a purpose to this. She would learn to use this invisibility in different ways while she was here. She experienced a vibration so high that no one would see her. This was a skill she shouldn't need often, but a good one to have. If she tried to walk through a solid, denser, lower vibration object and she kept her vibration high and held it, she would pass through a wall or an object. They would practice all this for as many days as they needed. It was one of the most advanced levels.

The sun was going down; they packed up their backpacks and returned to the cave. They had food waiting for them. Gracemama said they should put their packs outside their cave and someone would replenish their supplies. As Hope slept tonight, Gracemama said she would absorb everything she had learned. In the morning, they would return to the area and repeat the exercise.

After a few days of practicing and raising her vibration, Gracemama took her to a shelter not far away. They walked into the structure and then exited and walked around it. They stopped outside the wall, and Gracemama talked her through remembering her touchstone place to raise her vibration to a high level. Hope closed her eyes and remembered the sights and sounds and her song. She experienced that sensation she had become familiar with in the last few days. Her body felt tingly, similar to pins and needles, her hands and feet, legs, trunk of her body, neck and head, arms, fingers, and toes vibrated, and the sensation increased. Gracemama had her right in front of the wall. She didn't want her to open her eyes yet. This would come later. She told Hope to walk forward slowly. Hope did as requested. Gracemama kept guiding her and instructed her in the gentlest voice. Hope heard the flutes, her song; it brought her joy. Gracemama wanted this music embedded in her mind so she could bring it up whenever she needed to hear it. This music raised her vibration even more. Hope continued to glide forward and in the quietest whisper, Gracemama told her to stop and stand and then open her eyes. She obeyed. She was inside the shelter. Gracemama told her to hold her space, her energy, her vibration. They had spoken enough, so Hope understood what she meant. She told Hope with eyes open to do the same. Hope walked up to the wall and when her body was against it, she experienced resistance. Her vibration had slowed. It was because she had dropped her vibration with thought and surprise because she had passed through the wall. Gracemama explained what had occurred and then talked her through it back to how to regain the correct vibration. Then Hope tuned herself out and reached for her touchstone of the place with the furs and the music and the butterflies and the birds. The happy, joyful emotions returned and then she moved forward and into the wall, and through the wall and out the other side. She stood for the longest time. Gracemama had a drum by her which she beat with a slow rhythm; it was a deep grounding sound. Hope felt her vibration slowing. She was coming back. The girl didn't want to; she liked this high vibration. To become physically solid, she must be present and grounded, that would accomplish her goal. She must return to a solid state although she enjoyed the other. Gracemama was proud of her. She had done well. This young girl did not understand the gifts and power she possessed. She was coming into her own. She was stronger than she knew. Gracemama could see her for who she was now and what she was becoming. They headed back to the caves. In the following days, they went back to the clearing and repeated the exercises again.

CHAPTER ELEVEN

Preparation

Finally, the time for Hope's journey had arrived. One night, they sat in the cave and Gracemama explained to Hope that she would need to go out on her own for a period of time. Despite her fears about setting out alone she chose bravery. Younger than most for a journey like this, Hope would need all the knowledge she possessed. Gracemama imparted blessings over her for a safe journey. Then the wise woman gave her the pendant she wore. It was even more detailed than the one she had given her with the map and jewels. This necklace contained other properties. It belonged to Hope now. The girl hugged Gracemama. Hope would cherish this time, and her beautiful gift.

Together they packed Hope's backpack which would have what she would need. It contained basic tools and herbs and some light food for daily snacks. Hope would have to get her own food along the way. If the pack became too heavy, it would tire Hope. She was strong and capable as she demonstrated in her time with

Gracemama. The pack contained the basics for any situation. She possessed the skill set now to find whatever she didn't have and needed. Gracemama took a good amount of time to explain to her where she needed to go.

Hope had learned and grown a great deal. She needed to remain away from her village to continue to learn. The amount of time away concerned her. She didn't know to what extent the darkness had progressed. Gracemama explained to her now that she kept an eye on her village, her family and the villagers. Mother was mighty and done an amazing job with her sister, and some others, to keep the hope alive that they could save the village. Hope must take this journey. Gracemama communicated with her mother Jewelmama, and her mother reassured Gracemama that Hope needed to complete the journey, and then she would be ready for what would come. She would return then. The darkness was evil. No matter how much time passed, if Hope wasn't prepared there was no point as she wouldn't be strong enough, powerful enough. The decision settled. Hope would go on her journey.

She had been a good student and paid close attention. Her growth occurred in all areas balanced as it should be. Hope's physical size and knowledge in all areas had increased. Gracemama recognized she was ready and up to this test. It was time to sleep now, she would leave in the morning.

CHAPTER TWELVE

A Personal Journey

Gracemama woke up Hope early. The two of them sat in total silence as they ate a hearty breakfast and drank tea together. It was a quiet moment rich with many thoughts. After they ate, they sat and prayed together once more. Gracemama hugged Hope tightly and kissed her on her cheek. She walked her to the cave entrance. Hope felt the imprint of that kiss on her cheek. This young girl who had become a young woman boldly took her first steps and headed out away from the caves on the path alone. She headed in the direction Gracemama had told her to take. As she did so, she stood tall and proud; one could see this.

Hope walked all day sometimes stopping to eat a tiny amount of food and saving the rest. She took a small rest midday closing her eyes and resting on her cloth a little way off the walking path. Even in the rest, she realized to stay alert. All was well this first day. The light dwindled as she came to her first resting place. Hope found the tiny marker that no one would notice on the side of the path because of Gracemama's detailed explanation. The girl turned into the woods on the right-hand side. After walking through some trees a few steps, a path appeared that one would only see if they realized where to look. She followed the path for a minute or two and found the clearing and then her destination. It was different being alone. She studied the area and noted everything Gracemama described to her. Everything was there with the fire pit in the middle. That was the first thing to attend to. It was still light. She didn't know it, but Gracemama watched over her. She walked out of the clearing to a spot Gracemama told her about. Hope cleared away the leaves and branches. She walked back to her pack where she had a small tool to dig with. Next, she stepped back to dig about a foot down at the spot she had found. She spotted a container, a box with a lid. Hope pulled the box out and took the lid off and found supplies and dry food. She brought the container back to the fire pit after covering the hole leaving the dirt loose because she would return the box to its spot later. The sun was going down gradually, but she needed to get things done. In the box, she found dry tinder to get a fire started. Next, she found a few dry branches. Hope found a piece of flint and started a fire. She appreciated the fire was the most important thing to keep her warm and to ward off animals. The girl had been practicing and become adept at getting a fire going. Hope then got dry grain out and made a porridge. She seemed much better having some warm food in her tummy. After eating, she set up her simple but warm bedding. She prayed in thanks for her meal and a safe place to spend the night. Darkness set in, Hope lay down and fell into a deep sleep.

Her day had been long. She walked far and experienced a lot of emotions at the newness of being alone and separate from Gracemama. As Hope drifted off to sleep, she dreamed. In her dreams, her mother and sister came to her. They spoke with her and let her know they were all right and they would be there if she needed them. Her mother told her the village was growing deeper with darkness, but they still kept some light. They told her to do what she must so that when she returned, she would be strong and ready. Then she dreamed of the beautiful place she and Gracemama had gone to. She saw Gracemama in that place. She heard her song. The song helped her drift into nothingness and a peaceful sleep for the rest of the night.

Early that morning, she awoke and made porridge again. She returned everything to the container and put the box back in the spot and buried it again. She cleaned up the site. Her fire was small; there had been enough heat to cook. For safety, she covered the fire with dirt and packed her things and left. The place looked as it did when Hope arrived, just as Gracemama had taught her. The girl knew this was important.

Hope got back on the path and as she walked, she passed a creek about midday with berry bushes. The girl took a break and picked and ate many berries. She filled a container with water and also drank straight out of the creek. The water was fresh and delicious. The water flowed over rocks and pebbles which filtered it and made it pure. She felt strong and refreshed and continued on her walk. The trip would be one more day after this until she arrived at her given destination. She checked in with herself; she was doing ok.

Hope walked on. About mid-afternoon while passing through woods, which had been quiet, she began to pick up noises. The sounds made her stomach knot. It sounded like animals walking on dry leaves. She continued to move on along the path. At some point, the forest got darker and thicker. The canopy of trees kept the light out. The dim lighting made seeing difficult, so she tried to tune into her senses. Hope walked carefully so she wouldn't trip. She stopped and stood for a moment. The girl did not like the darkness which was eerie. In a flash she remembered what to do. The technique Gracemama taught her would also expand her light. Hope stood still for a moment using what she learned and grew her light. She focused on her heart and love. The girl thought of her touchstone, which Gracemama had shown her how to tap into. Then she heard her song in her head and hummed the melody. She chased the fear away by doing this exercise. She relaxed into the moment. The noises moved away.

Hope walked out of the thick forest. When she emerged, the sun shone, and it was a beautiful day. She needed a rest, so she looked for a good spot. Hope wanted to be away from the forest, so she walked for another half hour and then found a small clearing. Hungry for a snack she sat on a smooth rock and went into her pack for a little food and drink, then took a short rest on the rock. Warmed from the sun, she dozed. When she woke up, she felt better. She closed her pack up, got back on the path, and resumed walking. Her next job was finding the marker for the night. Gracemama told her along the way to look for the natural markers. When she did not find the spot she would spend the night at, she worried. She got hold of her emotions as she realized that would solve nothing. She regained her composure, and once again stood tall and proud as she walked. On the lefthand side along the path, about an hour before the sun set, she found the marker. It was a repeat of the night before, past a clearing through some trees and beyond a short path there was a buried box with supplies. She made a fire, ate, and slept.

Again, Hope woke early in the morning. She felt good from her sleep and the night had been uneventful. The girl continued on the trail. This should be her last day until she arrived at her destination. Hope continued at a steady pace hoping to arrive earlier than the last two nights. She decided not to take a break mid-morning and just go till midday and then stop for a break. Hope pushed herself but succeeded. She found a nice little clearing near a brook and sat down. Hope closed her eyes for a moment and listened to the running water. It was peaceful. She saw a few fishes swimming. Some flowers bloomed nearby. A little way off from where she stopped she saw berry bushes and picked some. She was tired and glad to have food. There was a little dried meat in her pack. Hope decided she needed protein to sustain her for the walk ahead. She broke off a piece and chewed it appreciating that this animal gave its life to give her energy. Hope prayed over the food. She spread out her cloth to sleep a little. The girl laid down curled up in a ball and fell into a deep sleep. She did not keep her guard up the way she had before because she let herself get too tired.

There were noises around her, but she didn't hear them. Animals came close to her. She continued to sleep. They moved in close to her pack. They were cats of some sort. Not huge, but big enough and in a group. The one close to her pack sniffed it and caught the aroma of dried meat. It stuck its nose around the tightly shut opening, trying to get it open. Hope awoke from the sound. She kept still and realized that an animal was close to her. She heard the noise of it trying to dig into her pack. Hope opened her eyes. She looked further away there were other cats watching the lead cat. They did not look nice or friendly. Her brain raced, and she tried to think of what she had learned. She did not have a tool or weapon handy. Instead of succumbing to fear, she thought of her touchstone; the place Gracemama taught her to go to grow her light and become invisible. She stayed huddled up in a ball the way she'd been sleeping. She didn't want to move or make a sound that the animals would react to. Her body vibrated. The sound of her song played in her head; she vibrated at an even faster rate. Then she disappeared. The cat saw her body lying there. It saw it disappear and got spooked, frightened. It pulled its head up and looked and then turned and ran away. When the lead cat ran the pack followed. They ran fast and far. Hope got up right away and was thankful she did not lose food or supplies. She needed to be alert. These were her only supplies right now to survive.

Hope got up, put her cloth in her pack and took off walking at a brusque pace. The girl was not paying attention. She turned the wrong way on the path and didn't notice she walked back the way she had come this morning. Hope walked for a good bit until she realized that she traveled in the wrong direction. The girl clued in when she saw familiar landmarks she passed before. She got her bearings and turned around.

85

Now Hope headed in the right direction. After walking a while, she passed the area she had rested. She kept on her way at a brisk pace. On she continued. Hope did not stop for her late afternoon break. She kept on walking. The girl became a little frustrated as she realized that she rested longer than she should have, in addition to walking in the wrong direction. This would delay her arrival at her destination. She might have to spend the night somewhere unplanned. This concerned her. As she walked, she talked with herself. *Now I must learn from this that I must always be aware even if I am resting. I must pay attention to my surroundings.*

Hope reviewed what happened. She acknowledged she handled the cats well, but still, they snuck up on her. The girl would have lost her most precious possessions, her food, water, and things she needed to survive. Hope would not let her guard down again. She must learn from this experience. The sun was going down. Hope became fatigued and hungry. Gracemama had described markers she would pass so she would recognize her progress on her walk. The girl would also realize how close she was to her destination. She saw the terrain change several times and Hope recalled Gracemama telling her about those changes. She realized she had further to go. What should she do? Hope decided with the darkness setting in and her tired body she should set camp somewhere for the night and complete her walk tomorrow. The girl experienced disappointment but understood it was not a good idea to keep going. She kept her eyes sharp and looked for a safe place as she entered an area where the girl saw a cliff on the right side. Hope discovered an opening in the sheer wall of the cliff. It looked like it may be the entrance to a cave. She realized there might be animals living in there, so she would need to be cautious. If she checked it out, it might be a good place to camp for the night. She moved to the opening and listened. It appeared to be silent. She took a step in and listened again. There didn't seem to be any noise. The area appeared to be a small cave with an opening at the top which would let light in. She observed it was empty. There were some large rocks just inside the entrance. Hope looked around to think. She would gather wood to make a fire if she hurried before dark. The girl had her tinder in her pack. She would dig a shallow hole in the center and build a fire which she would surround with the smaller rocks. It didn't need to be deep. Then she would shut herself in with the bigger rocks, build a door at the entrance so she would be safer. The smoke would leave out the top. If she kept the fire going well, it shouldn't get too smokey. She needed to hurry, there wasn't much daylight.

Hope continued about her business and found some nice dry wood. She got extra wood because she wasn't sure how much she needed. Hope was dead tired but worked through it. She spotted fresh growth of herbs while she was gathering the wood; she gathered leaves and also some root plants. This was a bonus and would give her some other food so she wouldn't deplete her travel food. The girl heard water nearby but realized she shouldn't stray too far this late. She had just a little daylight left to finish. Hope got back to the cave and pulled out her digging tool and dug a small fire pit. Then she put wood in. Next she tucked a little tinder she retrieved from her backpack underneath the wood. When she lit the fire, it burned right away. The smoke traveled up the opening. Hope moved rocks of the size she could manage. She moved them toward the opening where she entered. She rolled them and closed the opening pretty well. Good, she thought this would keep her safe for the night so she would sleep. Hope understood she needed to get rest and regroup. It was quite a day. She was bone tired. She cooked her porridge and then fell asleep.

In the morning, the girl would use the other supplies she had gathered. Adding that to her food would give her strength. Hope could use what she collected for various tasks. Some herbs would be used in cooking and some to make a salve for first aid cream for wounds or soothing muscles. Hope spread out her cloth and covered herself with her light but warm blanket. She looked around and decided she had created a safe place for the night. She stoked the fire; it burned well and kept the space nice and warm. Fire shadows showed on the rock wall and looked beautiful. Satisfied she fell into a deep sleep.

As she slept, Hope dreamt. She dreamt of Gracemama and then of her mother and sister. Suddenly, she was transported to them. Gathered together, they wanted to meet and talk to her. Her dream took her to the touchstone place where she had previously honed her gifts. It looked just like when she was there only her mother, sister, and Gracemama sat in a circle and waved her to join them. Gracemama said they needed to talk to her. In the cave, it only looked like she was sleeping. Her dreamtime transported her spirit to this other place so she could talk with her loved ones. When she walked over in her spirit form as they all were and sat down, Gracemama and the others prayed and blessed this meeting. They first wanted to show her how she could come to this place when she needed to. It was a place of restoration and a place they would all come to for Hope, a safe place. They told her she had done well on her travels; they watched her. Gracemama told her to stay where she was until she received instruction to continue to her destination. There was something Hope needed to learn in this place. She had no prior knowledge, but they hoped she would discover this location. It was part of the test, losing her way and adapting. They didn't tell her that. After she left this cave, when she knew it was time to move on, and got to her end destination, they would once again tell her when it was time to return to the caves where she had parted from Gracemama. Her mother spoke to her about their village. She explained to Hope to take the journey seriously because she would need to perfect her abilities. Between herself and Faith and some others, a few bright spots remained, but the darkness was taking more of a hold. They discussed a few more things and then told Hope she needed to return to her body in the little cave. She would be clear when to leave this location. Hope hugged everyone, closed her eyes, and visualized the cave and her body sleeping, and she was back in it. She was still asleep and slept until morning. When Hope awoke, she had full memory of what had happened. Back at the spot where she had left Gracemama, her mother Jewelmama and Faith, the three stayed a while and talked about everything. When they finished, poof, they all disappeared. They returned to their bodies.

Hope woke up starving. She stoked the fire again, which had a few embers. She pulled out her cooking items and made warm water and mint tea with some herbs she had found. This tea helped with the tummy and gave one energy. Hope took the lavender she had found and some twine and found a place to hang it in the little cave. She looked around as it had been late when she got there last night. It was time to cook porridge. She added root vegetables and various herbs she kept in a pouch. Hope saved what she had collected for a healing salve the night before to use at another time and put everything in a safe place. Her breakfast was tasty. It was nice to have some warm tea. The girl got ready for the day. She planned on spending her time gathering more items for food and warmth, and she needed water. Hope then removed the stones from the entrance, banked the fire so it would keep the coals going, and headed out. The first thing she wanted to do was find the water. The girl heard it last night, so she walked a short distance and caught the sound again. Hope walked off the path to find it and stayed alert to keep her bearings. It was a short walk to the river. The river was not too wide but the girl could bathe in it. She would gather water now and catch fish at a later time. The girl had brought along a bladder from an animal. She filled it full to the brim with water. She had brought along a little bag of supplies which she dug out from her pack. The supplies included a plant that works to wash with called soapwort that creates foam like soap and a comb for her hair. Hope looked around for a spot where the water didn't run so rapidly and removed her clothes to bathe. It was cold and refreshing. She washed her hair and her body. Then she took her clothes and washed them. She had a simple change of clothes, which she put on after her body dried in the sun. She laid her clothes on a nearby rock. They would dry quickly. She would flip them over in a little while. Once she got out and combed her hair, she braided it so it would be out of her way to work. For the rest of the day, she gathered root foods and herbs and any healing plants she could find. She gathered a good pile of dry wood and some tiny branches for tinder. She didn't want to use all of hers up. Hope took everything back to the cave. She walked in the direction she had come. She got confused for a moment, so she stood still, gathered herself and then saw her tracks and identified which direction to take. It took a few trips, but now she had wood, food, and supplies. She didn't expect to be here long, but thought it wise to be prepared. Hope walked back and got her other clothes as they were dry and folded them to take back to the cave. Back at the cave she prepared a meal.

It was midday. There was a fallen tree by the cave with the sun hitting it. Hope brought her food out to the tree and sat and ate in the sunshine. She walked back into the cave. The surroundings seemed peaceful outside, so she entered the cave and lay on her sleeping blanket to take a short rest. Hope spent the rest of the day organizing what she had gathered and then ate dinner. As the day ended she walked into the cave, closed it off with stones, and got the fire restarted. The girl wanted to practice the new things she had learned. She sat cross-legged by the fire and took her mind back to the touchstone and her song. Hope started the process. Her body began to vibrate and lighten; the sensation grew. Gradually, she brought herself to vibrating so high her whole body became transparent. She became invisible. She advanced slowly towards the rocks blocking the entrance she walked through the rocks and came out the other side. Hope then passed back into the cave. Satisfied she decided that was enough for today.

She was tired. This was a big achievement, she had grown more than she knew.

That night Hope slept soundly and in the morning got up intending to practice again. She walked to the river after drinking a special nourishing tea. The girl wanted to fish for dinner. She used her hands first to catch one and then practiced with her sharp knife. She was satisfied after catching two fish. Hope slit the fish up the belly and gutted them right there. After fishing, she bathed and dressed in her other set of clothes. If she didn't, she would stink like fish all day. Not that it mattered, she was alone. She felt better; she liked to appear neat and tidy when possible; it was her way.

She traveled back to the cave and pulled out herbs she had picked and seasoned one fish and cooked it on the fire. Hope ate the fish; it was delicious. She took the other plants and hung them high from a branch and then left to hunt for a ground bird. She knew with ground birds she had to be very quiet and still, maybe for a long time. When she aimed at the bird, she had to hit it right on the side of the chest. She used her weapon and aimed carefully. It was difficult, she only got one bird, but it was a good size ground bird. She gutted the bird and pulled the feathers off. After cleaning it, she added herbs to the bird and fish sealing them in separate bladders. She would cook them later that day. After preparing everything, she took the meats to the river to store till evening. She dug a hole in the water put the bladders with the meats into the hole and covered it with rocks so that the water would flow over it. It would keep everything cold, which would preserve it. There was no way animals would smell it underwater. Hope looked for more root foods and herbs both to cook with and for healing purposes. She wanted to stock up and be prepared. It had been a long day; she moved back inside her cave, moved the rocks that closed the entrance, and got the fire going. The fire gave her a nice warm light to work by picking the herbs off the stems. She cut the mint off the stems to chew on and freshen her mouth. She would make a tea from the leaves and the stems and use everything she could with no waste. After working for a while, she curled up and drifted off to sleep.

Hope awoke bright and early and moved through her daily ritual. Dressing, prayers, and food were the first activities she would do for the day. She removed the rocks at the entrance and walked to the river. The girl liked the river, so she walked there to find a spot to sit and meditate quietly. She took her time. On her way, she took in the beautiful aromas of the flowers in bloom along the trail. They were the sweetest smell she could remember. Picking a flower she put it close to her nose and from the scent thought the flower might be honeysuckle. She remembered it. A few flowers went into the small bag she carried. The bag woven from jute was to be worn over the shoulder, across body and hang to collect small things. She continued on her walk every so often noticing something she would pick up for use later. She arrived at the river. The sun was shining, she could sense it on her body. The sky was the most beautiful blue. She walked along the riverbank for a while and found a clearing on some flat ground just above the river. Here was a nice huge rock warmed by the sun. It had a flat top that looked perfect for sitting on. She settled herself in and sat and emptied her mind of thought. Her eyes closed, she appeared peaceful.

Hope's intention this day was to see if she could contact her mom and sister. She hummed her melody. It put her in a peaceful state. Then she stopped. She visualized her mother and sister in her mind's eye. Their faces appeared warm and loving. She could tell they saw her. She asked in her mind, "Mom can you see me? Sister Faith do you know I am here?" They smiled and nodded. She spoke to them through her mind and told them she was honing her skills and would contact them again when she needed to. Her mother and sister blew a kiss, and they vanished. Next, she contacted Gracemama. Gracemama came in clear. Hope asked her if it was time to leave yet. Gracemama said yes tomorrow morning at early light. She told Hope she should pack up tonight and be ready to go. The place had served its purpose. After the meeting Hope disconnected from Gracemama.

Hope sat on this spot; next she practiced expanding her light. If anyone had been watching, they would have been awestruck. Her light became so bright it was blinding. She expanded it very far out in a circle above, below, in front, and back like a globe. It traveled above the trees, across the river, back to the cave, and below the earth. She held this expansion for a while to make sure she could hold this state if she needed to. While doing this, her face became angelic, she looked so beautiful in this light, so powerful. Hope didn't completely understand how capable she was, but she was starting to. Everything she touched by her light glistened as though it was brand new. Next, she decreased the circumference of her light and brought it back into her natural state. She did this in a calculated manner. She wanted to be sure she could control her light, and if she wanted how far out it reached. The light expanded when she was in a certain state. Hope sat on the rock for a while longer looking at the surrounding ground and noticed a shiny clear crystal. She got up and retrieved it. It fit in her hand, it was a good size. She received a vibration from it. Hope sat back down and was quiet. The rock buzzed, and she saw images. She went no further with it but knew she would keep this crystal, it was special. She was getting hungry again, so she walked back to the cave.

Hope knew she was leaving in the morning. She had a short rest. When she arose, she would organize. The girl would leave early and she wanted to be ready. It might be a late night, she wasn't sure. She had brought back the meat, and she cooked it. She ate a good deal of it and hoped the remaining would keep till morning when she would eat the rest. It was a lot of food. Next, she took care and organized everything, and fixed the cave so that when she left, no one would know she had been there. Hope left the fire pit ready for morning. She also walked out to the path and made a marker that no one would notice. The girl didn't know if she would need this spot again on her return. She would tell Gracemama about it for any other travelers. The cave was ready to go by the time she laid down to sleep. One would never know someone had been here. She would cover the fire pit after cooking the rest of her meat. Then in the morning, she had a tree branch she would sweep her way out and back to the path so that her footsteps wouldn't even show. She slept, no dreams, and awakened refreshed at early light. Hope got up quickly. The girl ate the rest of the meat. She covered the fire so it would smoke out and left.

CHAPTER THIRTEEN

An Injury and a Meeting

As Hope began the last leg of her journey to her destination, she kept a nice easy pace. She learned if she rushed or walked too fast, she would burn herself out and get tired, and that led to errors. She paced herself. After walking for a short while, she came into an open area dry and devoid of growth. The sun beat down. The trail became hard packed dirt with desert like terrain. After a while, the ground sloped upward at an incline which steadily grew steeper. The path grew narrow and rocky and the terrain change became difficult to navigate. The trail switched back and forth, and some of it was composed of smooth rock and had no dirt. She remembered Gracemama described this area, so she acknowledged she was on track to her destination. She realized she still had some distance to travel. The trail was steep and narrow with one side of the cliff's edge dropping off with no view of the bottom below. The sky became gray as the air turned cool. Clouds rolled in.

Hope was halfway up the mountain. Turning back was not an option. She became a little nervous. Thunder and lightning became constant. The clouds and sky grew darker. The rain started first as a sprinkle then increased and turned into a downpour. She kept moving but did not rush. The path became hazardous. The girl's hair and clothes were soaking wet, with her hair flat to her head. Hope became cold and shook. The trail turned slippery, Hope tried to be careful. Her stomach churned; this experience made the girl tense.

The event happened so fast. Hope hit an extra slippery spot and and fell. Her ankle twisted hard. She fell down on a narrow part of the path. It hurt. Hope was in pain and when she looked down at her foot she recognized blood. Next, she found a wound on her leg.

Soaked and cold, Hope shook and grew anxious. High on this ledge, she realized if she slipped or fell again she risked going over the edge. The drop appeared endless. At the spot she fell the trail was narrow. The girl talked to herself, thinking out loud to keep her wits about her. She wouldn't stay here and became doubtful at her ability to walk. Hope found a handhold on the mountain side after looking around and took hold of it. She tried to pull herself up. She used her good leg to stand on and once she stood up, gradually put weight on her other leg. Instantly, she fell back down. As Hope held on to a little protuberance of the rock she tried again. This took all of her strength. She pulled herself up to a standing position putting weight on her good leg. Ok, *deep breath* she said to herself, *you aren't in a rush.* Hope still wore her backpack. She considered she remained in one piece. She watched blood dripping down her leg, but couldn't do anything about that right now. The smell of blood attracted animals. She knew this for sure. The girl wondered how she would get out of here. Her ankle looked badly sprained. When she tried to put her foot down and put weight on it her ankle hurt. She pulled her foot back up off the ground. Hope clenched her teeth and placed weight on her foot again. She didn't want it to give out, so she would have to walk at a slow pace. She took a step, then another. The pain became excruciating. Her ankle became increasingly painful as tears ran down her face. She kept going, limping; she must be careful not to make a misstep. After a little while, she rounded a corner. The path grew wider. The rain continued, the lightning thundered. She continued for about five minutes when she noticed an overhang of rock and opening in the mountain. The opening, fairly large, looked like the mouth to a cave. She knew wild animals might live here, but hoped not, as this would be a perfect spot. She knew she needed to find out if the cave was empty. This place would be a place to regroup even if just for a minute. Hope got to the overhang, the rain still pounding down. With the overhang the rain didn't reach all the way in against the mountain. She hobbled into the cave just a little. She didn't want to surprise any animals inside. The cave appeared dark inside except for the tiniest bit of light coming in from the outside. Hope heard no sounds as she stood and listened for a minute.

Hope sat down in a spot by the entrance and watched the pouring rain. She did not remember ever being this cold. The girl tried to calm herself down. Her ankle throbbed. How would she continue her walk to her destination? The girl worried.

Then Hope remembered all the healing herbs in her pack. She had something for this specific to injury, sprains or bruising. Her pack contained cloth to tear or cut into strips for her wound. The cloth would help support her ankle. She dug into her pack feeling around to the bottom where she stored her supplies. Hope pulled up a small bag. While doing this, she remembered how important it was to stay alert. Hope dug her knife out and placed it beside her. Her knife would serve two purposes, one as a weapon and also to help tear the fabric into strips. She also pulled out the fabric she would use for a bandage and wrap. Hope cleaned up the blood from the cut with water. She got out a special flower called arnica she had collected. Hope had leaves and the tiniest amount of oil. She also readied salve that Gracemama had sent her off with. Next, she would take her cloth and make long strips. Spreading a little salve made with arnica over and around the wound and the injured part of her foot, the girl was done for now. She would watch how her injury healed. The gash appeared deep and might leave a scar, but she had no way to close it except the cloth. When Hope wrapped her ankle, she held the laceration together at her ankle to squeeze and close the wound. It was painful and she winced but continued. With the other hand, she laid the end of the cloth on her ankle. The salve held the cloth in place so it didn't move. The girl did two wraps around as she let go of her cut. She continued to wrap tighter around the ankle and then got another strip wrapping under the arch of her foot. This made a sock type wrap that would close the wound as much as possible and provide support to her ankle. Hope did not want to waste or overuse anything. She would need the leftover leaves and oil to change the dressing later or tomorrow. When she finished, the girl inspected her work and was satisfied. Next, she took the arnica leaves and crushed them to break them up and give off their healing oils and properties. This is the way Gracemama taught her. She added them to the oil which she had separate. Bits of the flowers sat in the oil. This was not the way one would make it if time allowed and with the proper tools but it would work. What she made now the girl would use later to redress her ankle. This was the best she could do in this situation.

The rain stopped, and the sun came out and streamed into the cave. The space appeared to be large. She squinted to look back as far as she could. Droppings lay in the far corner, but they looked dry. She knew they would work as fuel for the fire and would be efficient. Near where she stood but in deep enough the girl spotted a small fire pit and a small amount of wood near it. She questioned who had been here. Animals will not go into their lair if a fire is burning. The animal droppings must have been left when no human was nearby. Maybe a person found it like her. They must have left wood behind and made the fire pit. Had someone lived here or just stopped off on their travels. Hope might never have the answer. Either way, she would not go further today. The path remained treacherous. And even though the rain eventually stopped, it remained extremely slippery. That is why she had fallen and gotten hurt. She pulled herself over to the fire pit with her arms and good leg and foot. She was near the pit and going to stay right there. The droppings looked too far away. She might collect them later to either use here or take along on her travels. It was light to transport, flammable, and created a quick fire. The droppings would be useful in her journey.

She took her pack off her back again and dug in to find the tinder. She found it and put it in the shallow pit. The girl spotted a few small, dry branches. They would work well. She put them on top of the tinder like a teepee. Hope kept two rocks made of flint. She struck them together as she had learned. After a short amount of time they sparked and when they did, the tinder went up into a flame quickly. She blew on it and it caught fire, burning one branch and then the next. After, she took a small sized log and placed it and another on top. The flames mesmerized Hope. She was fatigued.

Bringing herself back, she realized she still must stay alert. She didn't know what would wander into this cave. The light was going down outside and the flames danced off the walls. The smoke seemed to wander out through the entrance. Hope got out her cooking materials. She brought water from the last spot. Hope made tea and a simple porridge after spreading out her cloth. She was dirty from dragging herself but she didn't care at this point. What could she do about it? The girl shrugged her shoulders unconsciously reflecting that thought. She ate, and it warmed her on the inside. Her hair dried from the heat of the fire. Next she put two logs on the fire and prayed no animals would come in during the time she slept. She was aware she might sleep deeply. Hope applied salve to her ankle again and re-wrapped it with the same stripes. She lay down and slept immediately.

Hope's sleep was fitful with dreams that brought fear. She dreamt about a darkness and animals being around her and sat up from her sleep suddenly. The first thing she noticed, her throbbing ankle. Then she realized the darkness in the cave, the girl saw nothing because the fire had burnt down and was almost out. She took two more logs and placed them on the fire and hoped they would catch and burn. Hope noticed hot coals in the fire pit. The cave being so large the only warm spot existed right near the fire. She listened for any noises and looked around, she only saw the outline of the cave opening. Once the logs showed signs of burning and she heard no scary noises, she laid down and returned to sleep. Her sleep now deeper and more restful.

In the morning, the light streamed into the cave. It came all the way into her sleeping spot by the fire. Hope put her arm across her eyes and closed them again just to get her bearings. Then she remembered she was in the cave and had hurt her ankle. It all came back. She sat up and shifted so that the sun wouldn't be in her eyes but would warm her body. There was still a nip in the air as it was early morning. Next, she looked around and reassessed the cave. She found her wood supply diminishing. The fire was almost out; she threw one of the smaller logs on it after adding the tiniest bit of tinder from her pack since there were no more sticks. The tinder provided the flame needed to get the log going. After a while, she added another log. Hope thought thank heavens this place appeared to provide her shelter in her hour of need. Once she realized this, she prayed and blessed this place and gave thanks for it as she realized Gracemama would have. Hope didn't know what she would have done if this shelter hadn't been here.

She was surprised when she moved her ankle a little because it flexed and didn't hurt much. Her tummy rumbled from hunger. Since she was so close to the fire, she ate. Then she would test her ankle. After that, she would re-wrap it. She would use salve and the strips of cloth that remained. Hope would clean and redress the wound. She got her supplies and porridge out. The girl also took out ground vegetables she had collected and some beans for protein. It would be a good breakfast to sustain her. Hope didn't know what would come, and she needed her rest and her strength and to stay alert for the rest of the trip. She was in a cave and a human had been here or there would not have been a fire pit and wood. The girl was thankful for the scat; she reminded herself that she could use it here or pack it up and take it. It was light to travel with because it was dry. It showed that an animal had been here at some point. After Hope ate a hearty breakfast, she took out her supplies and the little water that remained. She drank some and then wet a small piece of cloth to clean her wound once unwrapped. As she unwrapped her ankle, she looked it over. The wound had closed up a lot and looked good. There was a little bruising, but nothing compared to if she hadn't had her salve. She moved her ankle and rotated it. To her surprise, she confirmed improvement overnight. Hope learned well what Gracemama had taught her. The salve and everything she did caused the injury to heal so well. She wiped and cleaned up her ankle with the wet cloth. The girl applied the salve using the amount called for, no extra, and re-wrapped the wound with fresh strips.

There was no room for waste because this was all she had for now. Hope understood how to make more salve but needed to find more flowers of arnica to accomplish this. The wrap would provide support to her ankle when walking. Hope took another part of the cloth and put water on it and washed her face, combed her hair and took out the other clothes that were clean and dry. Hope would keep a clean pair of clothes available when possible. Feeling better, she would attempt to stand. She boosted herself with her arms halfway up to her knees. Next, using her good foot the girl boosted herself up to a standing position. She carefully put weight on her injured foot. She stood quietly. Hope tried to sense her body, her leg and ankle. In the slowest way possible, one wouldn't even catch, she increased the weight on that foot. It was the tiniest bit sore. Hope took a step. This process went slowly; she was testing to gauge how her ankle was. It remained achy but improved. Then she repeated the process until she walked a slow circle around the fire. She would have to be mindful, but she could walk. It was amazing how much her ankle healed overnight.

Hope decided she needed to look around and decide what to do next. Would she move on or spend another night in the cave? If she walked well enough with the pack, she would move on. She didn't know what animals would come back to this cave if any. She would go to the cave's entrance and determine what was what. If she moved on, she would collect the scat, and try to replace some wood. As she learned from her teacher Gracemama, she would leave it as she found it, so that no one would detect she had been there. Hope was still standing and comfortable heading to the mouth of the cave. She took her time and moved about with just a little pain. Once again she marveled at how effective the salve worked.

When Hope got to the mouth of the cave, she discovered a beautiful day. The sky was blue. Everything seemed brighter after the rain. One might smell the moisture in the air and see the fresh green shimmer on the leaves of the trees. From where she stood, the view allowed her to see miles away over the terrain and down below. She would head up the mountain not down. The view over the land showed where she had come from. The path heading up the mountain looked like it was almost dry from the soaking rain. Hope looked to the left where she would head and saw the path got wider and spotted a few old looking trees. There was a little wood on the ground. She looked down the hill from where she had come to the right. Hope identified the path as it wound around the mountain and became much narrower and steeper. It appeared it was less steep the way she would go, at least from what she could see. The path seemed to level out, then disappear around a curve.

The trip took much longer than expected. She had run into little, no people and few animals along her journey. Hope decided she moved well enough to go on her way. The girl got lucky she had found this cave. She moved back inside to collect the scat. Then she would pack her things and cover the fire so that the embers would go out. After that she shuffled to where she had seen the trees. On the ground where she saw pieces of wood, she collected some. The girl took a few trips. When she discovered this place, it had been a God send to her and she hoped it would be the same for someone else. If the cave had not been there, she doesn't know what she would have done. Once the wood was back in order, she put her backpack on. She had found a branch coming off a tree with leaves on it that looked like a good stick to sweep her way out of the cave. She broke it off the tree with a crack, then as was customary thanked the tree. It almost seemed to answer back. That was peculiar. She continued about her business back in the cave sweeping her tracks on the way out so that no one would know she had been there. The rest of the path was more rock than dirt, so she would not have to continue to sweep the path too far, then she would toss the branch over the edge.

When Hope headed out, she passed trees; she swore they watched her. It was a strange impression, so she kept alert. Her senses proved strong right now. From time to time she seemed to hear nature speak to her, trees, rocks, and so on. After walking a while on the more level terrain where trees were growing along the mountain side, she noticed a branch laying on the path that appeared straight and sturdy. The branch would be perfect for a walking and it seemed special. The branch possessed an energy about it. Hope picked up the stick. The bark had fallen off. Hope moved her hand along the smooth wood. She thought the branch proved a perfect height to use as a walking stick. The stick had beautiful lines and the upper part where her hand fit was perfect for her grasp. It narrowed a little at the bottom so it would dig and grip the ground. She took it along and once again thanked the trees for this gift. She had learned there was a give and take from nature. That is how she learned to live both from her mother and Gracemama. She continued on her way. The walking stick felt good and helped her with her ankle.

As she moved along, she thought of her mother, sister, and Gracemama, and all the women at the camp. She missed them. The girl missed their company and friendship. She had forged good friendships. She also dearly missed the great wisdom of Gracemama and her loving protective way. Gracemama accepted Hope under her wing without question.

Hope thought about how she traveled on her own. She needed to be strong. She continued on her way as the mountain curved to the left. The path leveled out and got wider for a while. Her ankle did well. A little sore but good enough to walk on and her walking stick aided her. The girl saw the path ahead grow steeper and a little narrower. She decided since it was about time for a break this would be a good spot to stop. The trail was wide enough, so she took her pack off and leaned it against the side of the mountain. There was a tree growing there and a nice stone beneath it that would be fine for sitting. She went into her pack and found some dried meat strips. It had a salty flavor. Hope had a little water left, she drank a small amount and hoped she would find some soon. She should have filled up before she left. The girl hadn't because there was weight to water and with her injury; she didn't want her pack to be too heavy. Everything she did was a choice and she had to make good decisions when out here. She would watch her consumption until she found a stream. Once finished, she leaned against the tree which the rock butted up to and closed her eyes. The girl drifted off to sleep. She wasn't sure how long but something woke her. Hope jerked her head forward with force, her eyes wide open. She was wide awake now.

Hope focused and heard something. Where was the sound coming from? It sounded like a digging or rustling. She looked around again. Her pack was on the ground where she did not see it very well. She crawled off the rock and froze. She couldn't believe what she saw. Hope clapped her hands with a fury and yelled. Here right in front of her, she found an animal with his nose just into the top of her pack. It was digging around. When she yelled and clapped her hands, its snout came out and it jumped back with a fright. It ran about ten feet away and then turned around. They locked eyes. It stood glaring at her and she at him. Both their hearts beat rapidly. She studied the animal. It was doglike/wolflike. He was beautiful. Hope didn't let her guard down. It had been trying to get at her food. Thank heavens she had woken up. No harm no foul. As she stared at the animal, she saw its muscles relax; she relaxed slightly. They studied each other. The dog thought she looked kind. Her eyes to her soul were beautiful. This was no ordinary animal, he sensed far beyond what he saw. She could do the same if she paid attention. As she studied him, she noticed he had the most beautiful ice blue eyes. They cut into her but not unpleasantly, rather in a way she felt she was being seen. His fur was the purest of white. He had spirit and wisdom, a knowing. He was a good size and looked like he would hold his ground. They stood like this for the longest time. She became more relaxed and they stared at one another taking it all in for what seemed a long time.

Hope thought. What if he was part of a pack? It would prove dangerous. She carefully turned around and, with her back to him, she had her guard up. He stayed where he was. Hope packed her pack, got her walking stick in hand, and prepared to leave. She turned in the direction she needed to go. When she took a few steps, so did he. She stopped and turned around. The dog had kept his distance but he had taken steps matching hers. She said boldly "go, go now" and clapped her hands. She tried to shoo him away. He ran back. Hope walked again, the same thing, he followed her step for step. Hope would not allow this. She saw a few rocks. She didn't want to hit him. The girl threw them his way and yelled, "Go away, go home!" Again, she worried he belonged to a pack. She couldn't imagine he was all alone and wondered why she wasn't afraid of him. There was just something about him. The dog seemed to want to follow her. As she walked along, they continued this game for quite a while. Hope could not shake him.

For now, she wondered if she couldn't shake him, what could she do? So, she would stay alert to the dog. He wasn't leaving it seemed. The incline got steeper and narrower as she continued on her journey. The walking stick was handy. Hope kept a good pace. She kept looking back at the dog. He kept his distance but continued to follow her. If she stopped, he stopped. It became a game and time passed quickly with the distraction. It also took her attention off her leg. Hope discovered the spot she looked for. The trail continued. There was a marker and some bushes grew into the mountain side. She stuck her head between them. She realized that she had reached an important spot. There were steps carved into the hillside just as Gracemama had described. Hope looked behind her, no dog. She thought, *good I lost him or he left.* She needed no distractions, so she was glad. Even though her ankle wasn't causing a problem on the trail, she realized the steps might test her injury.

CHAPTER FOURTEEN

Setting Up Camp

Hope took a deep breath and pulled herself through the trees. She went up the tall steps. The climb and many stairs challenged her. She took her time. The way was narrow but she managed with her stick and pack. After an exhausting hour of this, she stood at the top of the mountain. The ground was level where she came out, a nice place to rest. The view was amazing and continued forever. Hope was proud. The girl had traveled far. She found the marker, made the climb and got rid of the animal.

Her thoughts kept returning to the dog, and this perplexed her. Why would she care about an animal like this? Something was different about him. Hope saw he was pure and proud. She could not have experienced love to and from an animal, could she? No, Hope thought she couldn't have feelings or love for a dog, absolutely not. She decided she traveled too long today and her thoughts and feelings were getting muddled. These thoughts were crazy, love from a dog. The girl allowed herself a short break; now the time was getting late, she needed to get moving. The directions Gracemama gave her were clear at this point. She walked for about another hour and found the area she would make camp. She would find a specific spot to build a camp in the next few days. Hope didn't know how long she would be in this area. Gracemama said she would learn when her journey here ended and she could return. After this last test, she would go back to Gracemama. After that, she would return to her village to help them. She would have all the tools she needed at this point.

When Hope found the exact spot to set up camp for now, the light was diminishing. She would be out in the open tonight; the girl had no choice. She dug a fire pit and collected wood. The most important activity became starting a fire and eating. After that, she made up a sleeping spot and fell into a deep sleep. Hope dreamt of the seven women who included Gracemama, also Faith and mother. Everyone in her dream gave her a message of welcome for Hope. This place was sacred. They encouraged her because she had made it this far and had done well. The group was all in her touchstone spot with her song sounding in her head. Then as easily as they appeared in her dream, they drifted out of it. She had no more dreams. Hope slept peacefully for the rest of the night. There were no incidents through the night for such an exposed site as the women and the dog watched over the girl.

In this place, Gracemama, Mother and Faith watched over Hope as they did all along her journey. They provided a level of protection. At certain times they would let things happen because she needed the lesson. She didn't realize it, but the dog also watched over her. He did not leave her, but backed off and away, so he could watch her and make sure of her safety. He kept an eye on her from a distance. The time would come when they would meet.

At early light, she awoke. Hope's eyes opened. She detected mist in the air, like a dream. The weather brought back what she experienced during dreamtime last night. The fog grew and became thick as soup. She must be watchful. The fire still contained embers. The outside of the logs she left for the morning seemed damp but the wood still looked good. With confidence she would get the fire burning. She put tinder on and it caught quickly; the flames blazed up. The warmth felt good. Hope sat up cross legged by the fire and stared at the flames. The girl became hypnotized for a moment. Then she snapped back. She realized she should not daydream too much. Somehow she seemed safe at this moment in this spot. She dug around in her pack and prepared porridge she learned was about half gone. She would have to find another food source so she would have the porridge or some other grain she brought along for the return trip. Some other foods remained in her pack. She possessed a few root vegetables and used them in her breakfast meal. She made a cup of special tea as she thought she would need to be alert. After breakfast, she unwrapped her ankle to inspect. The girl detected no mark of injury at all, no bruising and no cut or scar. That is amazing, she thought. With all the knowledge she gained from Gracemama, she realized that she recognized instantly what to use. This plant was what she had needed for her injury. Hope left her mended ankle unbandaged and moved on in her thoughts.

Hope needed to think about the day and how she would proceed. The mist rose and before her eyes appeared the most beautiful place she had ever seen. There was moisture around. The leaves had little drops formed on them which glistened from the sunlight. Everything growing seemed green, vibrant and alive. Some beautiful unique flowers grew nearby in various spots. Some grew low and appeared to like the shade near mossy places. Others found a sunny spot and grew tall reaching for the sun. The girl spotted birds, butterflies, rabbits, and other wildlife. This place was alive with activity.

The girl drew her thoughts back to practicality. She realized she had to set up camp somewhere, and then gather food, wood, and find water.

She hoped she would locate a good place today and the rest would follow. The good news was, she loved this place; it calmed her. Something about it resonated with her here. This place was no accident.

Hope finished up her morning prayers and packed up. Next, she covered the fire but left it there. She didn't know if she would use it again. Hope stood up ready to go. She picked up her walking stick and headed out to explore. Walking to the furthest edge, Hope found a path. She followed it and heard water. This would be a good direction to take. Her supply of water was low. The path headed in that direction. It led through some trees which looked like a small forest. They were tall and provided a roof from the sun. Most of their growth and leaves grew at the top. After passing through the small forest the landscape opened up as she came out of the forest. In front of her she saw a short cliff with a waterfall coming down into a pool. The crystal clear water and surrounding area was beautiful. The waterfall splashed down and created a mist where the water landed.

Hope saw the sky up above and the pool below showed a few fish swimming around. She would collect water and bathe here, this was perfect. Next, she looked around after filling up her containers with water. She noticed watercress growing wild along one bank; it was one of her favorite flavors to put with her foods. Hope picked some. She found a few plants she would use in the same general area. She would pick the leaves off and maybe use the stems a different way. Maybe a tea. Hope knew her plants well now. From some plants she wanted the roots because they provided a vegetable or potato. She pulled them for another variation in her meals. The warm weather seemed comfortable here. Next to delight her, she found wild berry bushes. She had all she could carry and would come back later. Hope knew if she carried them with everything else she had, they would get squashed. She would eat them fresh right off the bushes. She popped a few in her mouth. What a treat, the berries tasted sweet and ripe. When she reached the other side of the pond, the trail picked up and she walked a little further. She came upon an area as she followed along the cliff wall that looked shaped like a horseshoe. Cut into that cliff wall at the back she saw a small cave, like a little room. It was shallow. The good news, she saw it had not been used. Hope found no sign that life had been here. It seemed to be perfectly carved out of the wall. This was a perfect spot. She could make it work. From the cave, she could see out. Nothing would surprise her here. It was like a protective wall that came out from the cliff. What she liked most was that it would allow her to have a good vantage point to see what was going on. It seemed like a little safe haven. She would stay here.

Hope took off her backpack and left it in the shallow cave, she did not unpack it. The first order of business was to build a fire pit. She built it out far enough from the mouth of her room not to send sparks or smoke her way and yet close enough to give off heat. The girl made the pit deep, and she found smooth round rocks which she surrounded the pit with. Next, she walked back out in the direction trees grew. A forest stood nearby in the direction she had not traveled. She wanted to explore her surroundings, and it looked like a place to gather wood. Hope traveled back and forth and built up a nice wood supply. The girl picked up dead wood, some smaller dry branches and some kindling of little dry twigs. She broke off branches that displayed green inside, not dead. This took a while as she had to separate them from the tree, but she did it. She took them back to the fire pit. Hope pulled out her knife and carved the greener branches and built a place to cook food over the fire. They would not burn well and would let her support food on them. Now midday, she ate some dried meat for energy. After that, she walked back to the waterfall and jumped into the pool after checking the temperature and depth of the water. The water was not too cold at the further edge away from the falls. Then Hope swam in and stood still in a shallow area. She had her knife in her hand and saw an occasional trout swim by. She had learned to be quick as lightning. The light hit the knife as she came down swiftly and speared a fish. She would make an official spear later, it would work better. Hope pulled the fish up and brought it to the shore. She said a prayer right away thanking the fish for feeding her and giving its life. She then cut the fish open straight up the belly. Next, she pulled all its guts out. Hope worked with care on a smooth rock just by the pool. The girl wanted to use every bit of the fish. She felt for bones in the meat and pulled them out and then filleted the fish. It would be delicious. Hope had a bladder specifically for meat. She filled it with water, dropped the fish in, and tied it tightly. Then she found a spot where she buried it in the water close to the edge and put rocks on top to keep the fish fresh for dinner. She would come again and fish more but she had other things she wanted to take care of. Next Hope needed to find pine trees. It took a while and a short walk but she did. She looked on the ground and found the pine needles she looked for. They would make a nice soft sleeping area and then she would cover them up with her sleeping blanket. Hope filled her shawl with pine needles and hiked back to her cave. The girl repeated this action over and over until she had built a nice soft place to sleep against the back wall. She laid down on top of her new, soft bedding. She smiled, good work, she thought. It would be much more comfortable than the hard ground.

It was mid afternoon. Hope had gotten dirty and dusty from her travels even thought she had gone in the water earlier. The day was warm, and the sun shone. The girl decided as a luxury to go back to the falls and wash her clothes and take a waterfall shower. She gathered what she needed and headed back that way.

Hope was lighthearted and hummed her melody as she walked. She arrived at the pool and put her things down on the bank. Hope took her clothes off. She had brought her sleeping blanket and shawl to wash. The girl knew the sun would dry them in no time. She washed everything. Gracemama had shown her soapwort. It contained saponins which are steroids that dissolve in water and create a stable froth. Saponins named from the soapwort plant (Saponaria) whose roots historically were used as soap. She scrubbed and washed her clothes. Next, she laid them in a pile on a rock and dove into the water. She held her soapwort up above her head and swam toward the falls. She hummed her melody in her head. Washing her hair and body refreshed her. Hope climbed out of the water and sat on a sunny rock. The girl hummed while combing her hair. She let her naked body dry in the sun. Then she put her other set of clothes on which she had brought along. The time came to get back to her little cave. Some tree branches grew out of the cliff and the sun shone on them. It was a perfect place to hang everything to dry. It looked funny everything hanging helter-skelter, but it worked for now. She would figure something else out later.

After everything had dried, she took them down and folded things neatly. She returned her clothes to her pack and spread her sleeping cloth down again over the pine needles. The girl liked the aroma of clean clothes. Now early evening, her stomach rumbled. Hope returned to the pool. She was glad to have a water supply so close. That was very important. This seemed like a good spot because everything was nearby. Back at her cave, she found a good flat rock with a little height. It was not too large. She lugged it near the fire and used it as a table. She took her water bladder out and spilled a little water on it to clean the top. Then she spread the fish filets on it and used cooking herbs she had and pressed them into the skin. She stuck a thin branch through the length of the fish carefully. Then she cooked it over the fire. The aroma drifted her way, and it smelled delicious. Next, she made tea and then cooked root vegetables which she put on another stick. She was famished. She tried not to gobble the meal down, and when she was finished, the girl felt much better.

Hope reviewed her day. She wanted to make sure she had gathered what she needed for a few days. Satisfied that she had what she needed for now and could relax for a while. Tomorrow was another day. Her bones ached from a good day of work. It was time to sleep. Hope settled into her pine bed and covered herself with her shawl. The shawl kept her warm, constructed of something that held the heat well and resisted the rain. Her sleep was deep.

CHAPTER FIFTEEN

Exposure

The sun came up and streamed into her new little home. The girl was all nestled in and cozy. She curled up tighter as if ignoring the day. She wanted to stay in here forever. Eventually, she gave in and stretched her hands above head and feet and legs long into a full body stretch. She let out a big sound, "Ohhhhh!" as if bringing her body to life. She gave in to sitting up, dressing, standing, and going through her morning ritual. Hope stoked the fire, she recited her prayers, drank tea and ate porridge. She was awake now. Her song became a favorite, and she hummed it while she moved about. Then ready to take stock of her day she would decide what she needed to do. Unloading a few things out of her pack, she dug a hole near the mouth of her little cave. She buried them and covered them with the heaviest stones she found manageable. This way she would keep her things safe and hidden when she traveled.

Occasionally Hope would leave camp. She would have to hunt and eat meat, birds or a larger catch. She would take it day by day. Today she would explore the area and hunt for a few ground birds for dinner.

Hope cleaned up and covered the fire with a little dirt to help it go out for the day. When she traveled she didn't want the smoke and the fire going. The girl had met no one yet. She started out walking to the waterfall to fill the bladder with water for her day trip. As she left the area, she walked in a new direction. The girl walked for a long time. The ground was flat as she emerged from the woods to a field. Hope looked around as she walked through the field. She found a spot where there sat a beautiful warm flat rock. Hope climbed up on it. The rock was high and gave her a good view of her surroundings. She sat on it in a hollow that fit her body.

The girl realized she needed to spend time out practicing building her light. She was here to learn. She shifted, getting into a comfortable cross legged position sitting with a straight back. Then Hope thought of her touchstone and her song and hummed it. The song had quite an effect on her light today. It grew strong around her body and expanded. It continued to grow. When she had gone as far as she could, she held the circumference of light around her and hummed. Slowly she brought the light back in close to her body in a controlled manner. She welcomed this experience and practice time.

Hope sat for a while on the rock. Creatures seemed attracted to the energy. She looked at the birds and butterflies. Her vision became sharper, and the plants seemed more vibrant. It seemed as if she created more life in everything. Her body buzzed with the energy. She had raised the vibration of her cells though she didn't know or understand the dynamics of what had happened. She only knew what she discovered from this experience.

From the higher vantage point on the rock, she could see the rolling terrain and mountains in the distance. Hope was hungry from the energy expansion. She dug into her pack to get food and drink. Once satisfied, she lay on the rock and rested a short while. This refreshed her. With caution, she climbed down putting her feet in the places that jutted out. It wasn't too far down, but she was careful. Her ankle and wound had healed with no sign of ever being injured. She didn't want to injure herself again.

Hope walked for the rest of the day stopping once in awhile and doing a smaller energy and light expansion. She knew this would be one skill she would need when going back to her home. She also practiced her invisibility. This was a harder task. She was improving. She found a tree and tried to pass through it. It took a while, eventually she succeeded and passed through again. This skill was difficult and advanced and the girl was young to be learning it. Hope was special and so were her talents, she had the ability.

Later in the day, she came to an area by a small pool of water. There were ground birds around. She got her weapon out. She saw a fluffy brown bird drinking from the pool. Swift as a rabbit she was upon it and killed it. Hope found another one when she was rounding the pool, and again swiftly she pounced and got this one. She cleaned both birds. Then she gutted and removed the feathers and wrapped it in a bladder. Hope had a loop on the outside of her backpack she hung it from. It swung as she walked but was secure. That would do for dinner. It was getting late. Hope ate a small piece of dried meat and headed back. She would continue to practice and master her skills.

Hope hurried as the sun disappeared. She traveled far today but remembered how to find her way back. Gracemama had taught her how to navigate. She followed the sun and paid attention to the terrain and occasionally would break a branch to help. In case she wanted to return, she would have markers. Hope wasn't to the waterfall yet, she still had a distance to go. She should have headed back sooner. The later it got the darker it grew and she couldn't see well. Her nerves were getting the best of her. Hope hadn't brought things to stay anywhere overnight. She got a little confused on the trail. Hope experienced relief once she got her bearings and heard the waterfall. As she came upon the waterfall, darkness set in, but she remembered her way. She caught two shiny eyes at the edge of the area. An animal drank water. It looked up and took off fast. She had her guard up and held her weapon. The animal ran fast and away. Hope was glad. She would build a fire to ward anything off and stay alert. Following the trail she had tread since her arrival, Hope made her way back to her camp. She was glad when she arrived. She felt safer. If anything entered, she would be aware and she would defend herself. Hope immediately got a fire blazing in her fire pit. She took the birds she had caught and rubbed them with herbs and skewered them. The meat cooked quickly. She made vegetables and tea and ate what she considered a hearty dinner. Her belly was full and satisfied. Tired, she fluffed up her bed, curled up and fell asleep.

Her mom and sister came to her during the night. They counseled her. She was doing well. They stressed to Hope that she needed to keep alert. The village had grown increasingly dark. Hope realized this when she communicated with her mother and sister. Light still emanated from Faith, mother and their home. Hope traveled like she did in her sleep sometimes. When she got to the village, she recognized their challenges. The people ambled, lifelessly and seemed almost dead. She flew over her Father, and he sat like a lump on the ground. The girl experienced sadness. He had been such a great man. There was not much life anywhere. Next, Hope left the village and flew over the caves and the place where she spent time with Gracemama at first. She then cruised over her camping area. The girl looked at her body sleeping and saw animals in different spots moving about in the night. Next, she saw a flash of white near her sleeping body but couldn't determine what it was. She didn't get the impression it was dangerous or after her. Far from where she camped, she saw a fire and a camp. Hope couldn't make out the people that were there. They were inside asleep. It was clearly a camp and looked similar to hers, larger and with some different features. It had the look of a work and hunting camp. Hope wondered about it and noted how curious she seemed about this place. She seemed drawn to it. The girl found no other camps or villages around and she covered some ground in her travels that night. She returned to this camp and hovered around it for a long time. Suddenly, she looked at a figure come out of a hut. The figure seemed stealthy and appeared to be moving about carefully. It looked like a person and moved around the huts and out of the village. Hope became intrigued and drawn to it. The reaction surprised her. She had learned discipline and realized this didn't need to be her focus now. She did not seem drawn to anything else. All the other things she passed over she just observed, except for the sadness she got from her village. She now seemed pulled back to her body. With the wisdom she gained, she gave in to that. Once back in her body, she rested until morning.

In the morning when she woke, Hope remembered the entire experience. Curiosity set in about the white flash. She looked at it and didn't think it seemed dangerous. The girl had learned to trust her feelings and instincts better. She thought about this other village, but she had no answers. Hope lay on her soft warm bed for a while. She felt safe here. Finally, she gave in to the day and got up. She walked to the waterfall and took a bath in the pool. She brought water back to her camp and made food and tea for energy. Hope decided she liked being alone. She enjoyed hearing nothing but nature sounds. All of her senses became more heightened every day.

Today, she would explore in a new direction. She hoped to gather food along the way. After she readied herself, she put her pack on and took off at a good pace. Hope packed all she thought she might need. Today she took her spear, and her smaller weapons so she might hunt, and as protection. She didn't need her walking stick any longer as her ankle and leg had healed.

The direction she took was new and opposite of where she went yesterday. Hope headed away from the waterfall on the other side of her camp. She walked all day. Hope got a sense eyes followed her. The girl realized something watched her. She stayed mindful and kept on her way. She carried her spear in her hand if she needed it. Hope had a place on her pack she could attach the spear if she wanted. Today she thought she should keep it in her hand just in case. She passed through thick woods, the path seemed well worn. It might be from the animals, she couldn't tell. Hope noticed droppings every so often. They were of different sizes which would mean various types of animals. She identified some as smaller animals and birds' droppings. Her hearing was sharp and would pick up the sound of creatures hopping around in the woods. Hope traveled well past noon. Typically, she would stop earlier, but today she wanted to cover some distance. She wanted to identify her surroundings. She still felt eyes on her, and found this curious because it was constant, but nothing came after her. It seemed like something or someone followed her and watched her. In the afternoon, she finally took a break in a woodsy area. The girl found a place off the path and cleared it. She took out her ground cloth which she brought with her this time and spread it out. She sat down on the cloth and ate a little and rested. Hope didn't let her guard down, it was a half sleep, so she would be alert. She still sensed eyes upon her, so she decided not to stay too long and chance falling asleep. After a short rest and food she packed up and continued on her way. The rest and food helped regain her energy. She continued on and passed a brook. She observed fish swimming. Good, she thought she would catch dinner here on her way back to camp. Hope discovered birds and ground squirrels along the way, and at one point she found a mama and baby deer. The wildlife was plentiful.

After a while she came to the end of the forest to a more open space. The area seemed high as she had climbed for a while. Hope had a panoramic view and saw the valley below. The sky showed gray clouds rolling in, she realized she must follow the weather. A river cut through the bottom of the valley dividing it in half. Hope viewed more wildlife in the valley. She stood right on a ledge and experienced wind blowing through her hair. Down in the valley near the river, she looked at smoke rising. It looked like a camp. It looked like the camp she observed the night before as she traveled in a dreamtime. Hope detected movement. She asked herself, *did she need to worry?*

It was time to practice, and she recognized she was far away from the camp. She saw no other movement except in the camp. Hope sat down on the ledge and practiced the same way she did the day before. She wanted to enlarge her radius of light even further than she had previously. She practiced for a good long while. Hope was certain she wouldn't be noticed but she was wrong.

The camp consisted of all-male hunters. It was the one she discovered the night before. The figure she looked at the night before was a boy in training, who lived with the men since he was young. He liked to sneak out of the camp sometimes. This boy knew their ways and did everything they did but differed from them. He didn't like hunting. He had gifts he wasn't aware of, similar to Hope's, but didn't understand them so he dismissed them. Because of his sensitivity, the boy learned to be a good hunter, so the men thought just that.

Some men in the camp experienced an uneasiness noticing this strange bright light that covered the camp. They agreed to put a small group together and take the boy with them. They held no concerns. Hunters were strong and brave. This light remained unfamiliar, so they agreed to investigate.

The men and boy grabbed their packs which were always ready in case they left to hunt. It would be best to go right away. Their packs contained supplies to stay two or three nights. They had food and weapons ready to go. The group moved expeditiously as a team. They wanted to cover some ground.

When Hope finished practicing, they lost track of the light. The group remembered the general spot the light came from, so they continued until it grew dark. They had left in the afternoon. The men identified themselves as good trackers and would continue tomorrow. Wisdom taught them not to travel at night. They made camp.

CHAPTER SIXTEEN
Caution

After practicing, Hope headed back the way she had come. She wanted to get food during her trip if time allowed. Along the way, she found berry bushes and filled up her tummy. She smiled at the sweet flavor. Hope also found healing plants. She collected a variety and found a few new root foods. Hope also found fruit trees, she identified the safe fruits, and collected some. That was important; things might be deadly or make someone ill. Hope gathered all she could carry. She would find the brook and catch fish. The girl found her way. It was late afternoon; she hurried along. She grew hungry again. Hope became warm from walking when she found the brook. A rock hung over the water of the brook. Hope kneeled on it and hung her head over to look under the rock to locate fish. Next, getting down from the rock and entering the water, she advanced carefully as she had learned. The girl didn't want her shadow to scare off the fish. She carried her spear in hand ready to strike. The moment came as a large trout swam forward a little. The girl moved swiftly and speared the fish. She pulled it out of the water and said a prayer to thank the fish for its life. One fish would do. The day was getting late, Hope was uncertain she would get back to camp, so she camped here. She made a small fire and cooked her evening meal.

After eating Hope banked the fire. This would allow the coals to stay hot all night keeping her warm and making it easy to start a fire in the morning. She laid out her ground cloth and used her shawl for a blanket. She liked her soft bed back at camp, but considered her decision wise to sleep here. The sound of the running water lulled her to sleep as the eyes of the unknown surveyed her from a distance.

Gracemama came to her while she slept and seemed to be trying to tell her something. The wise woman had a stern face as she wagged her finger. Hope did not understand what the wise woman was trying to tell her. Next, as she slept, she saw the dog she encountered after she had her fall and injury during her travels. The dog looked soft and white, fluffy and loving. Her heart experienced happiness when she saw this. She slept on. Hope slept deeply and rose early. She enjoyed the sound of the brook when she woke up and hummed her melody. The sound of the brook and her song fit perfectly together. She washed her face at the brook, refilled her water supply, and rinsed her mouth. She ate a nice warm breakfast. This would sustain her for a good part of the day. She packed up her things and moved on.

As Hope walked, she continued to hum her song as she imagined her touchstone, unaware that her brightness emanated a great distance around her. The eyes that followed her were constant. Had the girl recognized this she would have had fear. She made good time and walked for many hours. The trail was narrow but smooth and not too difficult. Terrain changes took place in the trail she traveled. She remembered most of the walk from the other direction. At one point she entered an open area after walking a long time. Hope crossed to the other side and found a concealed spot at the perimeter of the forest to rest. She was tired and hungry after walking for so long. It was midafternoon. The girl spread out her ground cloth, dug into the bottom of her pack and found food. She ate the food and drank water. She laid down and rested. Hope fell into a deeper sleep than planned.

The hunters kept on. Far from their camp they had not reached the area where Hope had been practicing yet. The group headed toward her. When they reached the area, they looked at flashes of light in the distance. This made her easier to track. They saw some footsteps which appeared to be small. The group wondered who they tracked. They recognized these were not animal footsteps. The hunters found branches snapped off here and there. This was Hope's system to mark her way, not realizing others would use it to follow her.

The group arrived at the camp where she had slept. They studied it and found little trace of the girl. They knew competent skills when they looked at them as they were expert hunters and trackers. The small group ranged in age from the older Wise One to a boy about Hope's age. He was in training. Though they didn't talk about it, this is why they brought him. He would learn as he always did on these trips. Since water was here, they took a short break and ate. They didn't know how long into the day they would be traveling. This might be their only opportunity to stop. They found dried meat strips of jerky in their packs. This was standard and a great traveling food to get the protein they needed. Marinated in a sweet sauce before drying, the meat would keep a long time. Then they drank water from the brook and refilled their water containers. It was time to go. The boy and the elder man's pace was slower, so the men went at a slower stride so they could keep up. This was to Hope's advantage.

Hope snapped awake. She realized she shouldn't have let her guard down and slept so deeply. She sat up and spotted paw prints around where she slept. This concerned her. It appeared as if they came right up to where she slept. The girl detected no noise. She remembered her dream's visions and tried to make sense out of it. She recalled that Gracemama looked like she urgently tried to tell her something, but she didn't grasp what. Then her heart experienced love when she remembered the dog. Why did he keep coming up in her thoughts? She decided whatever Gracemama was coming to her about in her dream she better get on her way. While she walked, she would practice her skills as she had planned. Knowing how to shine her light while on the move was an additional skill. She didn't know when she returned to the village what she would encounter. She better practice everything. Hope didn't realize how much she had grown.

Hope walked at a good pace. She had a nagging sense something followed her, but she looked around and saw nothing. She didn't have fear. It seemed like something kept pace with her at a distance behind her. She saw nothing, so she kept on and kept alert. She paid attention as she walked on the well worn trail and entered the woods. Hope didn't want to fall again. The sunlight streamed through the trees. The forest was beautiful; it looked all lit up as she hummed her song and thought of her touchstone. Her light expanded around her as she walked. When she would stop humming, her light would pull in closer to her body. She continued through the forest.

The hunters were still a distance from catching up to her, but they were on her trail. The men talked about the small foot tracks and the light. What and who did they track, what would they find? They had no answer, but they would learn soon. They couldn't be that far behind. What they didn't realize was Hope hurried. She made good time. The group fell behind.

Hope thought about a course of action. What she might do about this nagging suspicion of something watching or following her, or both. She wanted to make it back to her place tonight. She also wanted to identify what might be going on around her. The girl didn't want to lead anyone or anything to the camp. She kept walking while she pondered this. Her heart beat a little faster as she realized there might be dangers lurking around. After walking for some time, she pulled off the trail. She would practice her invisibility that way she hoped to find out what followed her. There was a tight group of trees and she made her way into the middle of them so no one would see her. She must focus. She hummed her song in her mind so as not to make sounds. She envisioned her touchstone in her mind's eye but kept her eyes open. This sense that expanded her light was the easy part. Now she had to increase her vibration. She sensed her cells vibrating which was a good sign. Her body vanished from head to toe. Once she realized she had succeeded, she walked or passed through the small group of trees and stood in the open. She continued to hold her vibration. She heard the footsteps walking on the leaves and remained silent. Her heart beat fast as she stood out in the open and watched. Hope took this risk, and she didn't know what she would find. The footsteps came closer.

The crunch of the leaves gave them away. It crossed the path and came closer to her. What was it? She became frightened. It seemed like her food moved up into her throat; she thought she might vomit. Something came into view. It appeared to be looking for her and thought it sensed her. Then she saw it. It walked up to her and stopped. It looked up at her as if it saw her. How was this possible? She was invisible. Next, it sat down in front of her and then laid down. It watched her and looked directly into her eyes. Hope thought any person or animal would not find her. A dog stood before her, a big beautiful furry pure white dog. The one she had seen before. She remembered its eyes, blue like the bluest sky. Its fur white as snow. This was the same dog she had seen after her injury. She determined it had stayed with her all this time, secretly following her.

The girl slowed her vibration to become visible. Hope stood still. The dog did not move. They looked into one another's eyes for the longest time. Time seemed to stand still. How did this animal find her and track her without being seen? Why would this dog do that? Hope believed this creature would not harm her. She sat down. She reached her hand out to touch it. His fur felt soft, comforting almost. The dog didn't move. It licked her hand. When she put her hand on the ground, it put its paw on it as if to touch her or say hello. The dog seemed to communicate with her in its own way. She reflected on this animals beauty. Hope received tremendous love from this dog. She returned the love. It made a sound. Love came from this sound as if answering her. Hope stood up and as she did, the animal did the same.

Hope snapped back. She realized she better get going. For a moment she reasoned, maybe I will keep him; then logic kicked in. A dog would be a burden, her idea was silly. Hope petted his head and took a few steps to be on her way. The dog followed her keeping close. She realized her reasoning process, this was not a dog one kept. She sensed his love, but she also understood his power. He was his own master. Hope turned around and spoke to him. The girl took a chance he would understand. She said, "Please I am on a journey and do not need a companion, I am going now."

As she started moving away, the dog followed. She turned and shooed it, but realized that was all she could do. The dog persisted, just like before, and it continued to follow her no matter what she tried to do to shake him. Hope recognized the connection she had with him. She didn't understand, but she accepted it. On a heart level, she got it, but she didn't have time to bother with him any longer. She needed to reach her camp before dark. She would try to send him away at a later time if he didn't leave her. Hope walked with a determination to get back to the cave. The walk was long, but she made good time and arrived just before sundown. Her meeting of the dog delayed her trip or she would have arrived earlier. She readied her site with her fire and cooked her food right away. The dog, still with her, stayed close. She couldn't deny she liked the companionship. He didn't seem to be extra work. The dog was independent and had survived on his own. Then she reconsidered and told herself I don't need a dog. For now, she gave up thinking about it and got ready for bed after she ate.

Exhausted, Hope settled into her bed. She stared out of the cave opening. The dog lay near the fire sound asleep. She hadn't fed him when she ate because she didn't want him to stick around. The night was pitch black except for the fire. She heard all the sounds of nature around, and it calmed her into sleep. She stirred in the middle of the night uneasy as if something was coming. Hope again dreamed of Gracemama and sensed the warning. She wasn't clear on the message, but felt it in her gut. Hope woke up in the middle of the night. She slept on her side all cuddled in with her shawl on top of her. She noticed something in front of her in the curl of her body. Hope reached forward it was soft and warm, like a heater. She realized the dog had come to her while she slept and curled up next to her body. He slept soundly, and she curled into him. Having him there soothed her nerves and calmed her. Hope fell into a deep sleep feeling more safe and secure.

The next day, Hope ate her morning meal and shared some of her food with the dog. Then she practiced her skills. It was a beautiful day. She liked having his company. When she went to collect water, she washed her dirty clothes and took a bath in the pool at the falls. The dog followed her in. He was a good swimmer. She soaped him up for fun and washed him while she bathed. The dog got out of the water before she rinsed him. Hope called him back in and rubbed him down to get the soap out. The soap had a sweet smell, and now the dog smelled like it. She talked to him. He responded to her.

It was a full day. Hope was tired but knew she had to take care of practicing her skills. The girl would eat first and then practice. She was getting good at everything she learned. It was becoming natural to her. No matter what, every day she knew she needed to practice.

Hope was happy. She loved being out here in nature. That night, she gazed at the sky and the wonderment of so many stars. She heard the waterfall even though it was a little distance away. She sat by the fire petting and talking to the dog and humming her song. Her light grew bright even in the dark. It shone very far. The light stayed around her now unless she stopped it. She had grown competent in her skills. Enveloped in Hope's light the dog immersed himself in this loving light.

The hunting party followed Hope's trail, but they had fallen behind. They traveled until dark then pulled off the trail and set camp. The group made a quick fire to have a little food and sleep. They slept close together for the body heat. The fire blazed at first, but died down during the night, with just the glow of hot coals. They woke early, ate, and packed. One man covered the fire with dirt so it would go out. They swept their way out of camp as they left. The men picked up Hope's trail as morning broke. They tracked easily even with little sunlight.

The girl stirred. The dog was still by her side. Hope had an uneasy sense or premonition that something was coming. She realized that the dog gave her a sense of safety, like he would protect her. She didn't know why she thought this way, but she did. He seemed friendly and not a bother. She didn't want to ignore her premonition either. She would stay mindful.

Hope got up and stirred the fire. She threw a few tiny twigs on it and got the flames going, then a log so she could make breakfast. She knew she shouldn't, but she gave the dog a little food on the rock, which had a perfectly shaped dip in it like a bowl. The dog lapped it up. He looked at her, and she swore he thanked her. After the morning meal, she put water in the dip for the dog. She was very careful with her water usage, but she could spare it as she was going to the falls to replenish her water supply. Hope stayed by the camp today and replenished her supplies. Her anxiety persisted. If there was any merit to it, she thought she could protect herself here best. The dog followed her around all day. She collected a good stockpile of wood and found herbs and root foods. Next, she speared two fish which she gutted and cleaned. Once again she stored them as she always did in a bladder with cold water. She placed it under rocks in the pool to keep them cool until dinner.

Hope gave thought to how to protect herself here at her camp. All around the falls on one side where the water flowed into the pool, she found a bunch of tiny rocks. She collected as many as she could and took them to her camp. Her plan was to spread them across the entrance. The camp was a horseshoe shape. The open part was the entrance. She closed the entrance off with a bunch of gravel. Then she collected dry leaves to cover the gravel. When she stepped on it to test her idea, it would crunch. This should get her attention like an alarm and would alert her of any intruders. As a little girl, she had played with a slingshot and a target. It was a game she played with her friends in the village. Hope became a good shot. She needed to create a slingshot. The girl took a while to get what she needed and designed one. She used a wishbone shape of wood that was solid and wouldn't break. She had sinew which Gracemama had packed for her that would work to attach from one end of the fishbone to another. This would allow her to launch stones. Hope wove a sturdy basket where she would store stones. She would hurl them. The girl would keep these in her cave. She also had her handmade spear and made a couple more that she would launch. She wanted to have extras in case she couldn't retrieve them. Hope experienced fear by the premonition she received, but she knew this journey was for lessons. She must have courage and quiet the fear. Dog helped calm her by his presence.

CHAPTER SEVENTEEN

Finding Hope

The hunters were getting closer to Hope. They realized they continued to be on her trail. The search didn't seem as urgent now. When their hunt had been closer to their camp, pursuit seemed more pressing. Whatever they chased did not pursue them, it moved away from them. Because of the distance from camp, the threat became less.

The group included a boy, the same boy that the girl observed leaving the camp when she sat on the ledge. She only observed a shape moving, sneaking out of the camp. This boys hair and eyes looked similar, dark brown to blackish like hers. These men trained him since he was little. He worked hard at keeping pace with the men. He moved slower because he wasn't as tall as the men. They understood but sometimes got frustrated with him. Some hunters acted tougher with him, some more kind.

The hunters made camp after walking all day. Before going to sleep they ate and talked of home. They planned to leave early as they often did. They discussed the trip.

The men wondered, did they waste their time? They would decide in the coming days. Far away from their camp, the perceived threat should not be as great. The boy seemed restless and didn't understand why. He stayed awake with curiosity about the light they tracked. The boy didn't want to harm it like the men might want to do. What they didn't understand scared them. He experienced a light like this before. He didn't remember where. There was no discussion or nurturing of the abilities the boy possessed. As a result, he didn't understand. Only a few men at the camp suspected, but no one mentioned anything. He liked to track but not the hunt. It always seemed cruel. He didn't mind getting some immediate food, and he understood they hunted to have stock. The capturing of animals pained and saddened the boy. Sometimes when alone, he wept over the killings. Hunting did not belong to his nature. This was the way of these men and he understood he must follow what they taught him. They sheltered him and took care of him and took him under their wing like part of their family. He remembered little of his childhood before he lived at the camp with these men. He barely remembered his parents. While he sat, he watched the light again. Everyone slept. He wondered how the light shone in the darkness with all this beauty, reminding him of a seashell lining with a pale white sheen.

The boy basked in the light. The men slept and did not stir. He just sat and stared. Where did this light come from, with all its beauty? He enjoyed the love in the light. Next, the oddest thing happened. He picked up a melody, a beautiful melody. This too came from love. Where did it come from? It was familiar. As he listened, another odd thing happened. Small and close to his body a light emanated. This familiar phenomenon from his own light he recognized as love. The boy recognized and hummed the song. He didn't want to wake anyone because this would not be acceptable. These men only thought about survival and hunting. They cared for him, but this behavior would not work for them, this the boy realized. When he realized these emotions, his light drew in close to his body. He shut down when fear took over instead of love. The boy shifted his thoughts back to the light and love. He again hummed the tune low so no one would overhear. His light expanded. How did this come from him? He had never learned what to do and where this light came from. The boy was glad the men slept.

The boy didn't want harm to come to the light. He had an urgent duty to protect that light and whoever it belonged to and decided to leave that night. It was risky. The boy would see if he could track the light. He realized it was dark out, but he must try. These men might destroy it. The boy couldn't be sure. Once he decided, he packed up. He took food from a pack. The packs sat in a big pile. He took some dried meat, his spear and a sharp knife. He took everything he needed. The light shone on the path which helped the boy navigate. He had learned enough to follow the tracks. Fear would not stop him because he possessed confidence in what he now decided to do. He picked up a branch with leaves and used it like a broom. He drug it behind himself to clear his footsteps and the ones they had been following. The boy traveled as quickly as he could. He questioned his reasons for doing this, why he experienced this pull, but he believed he must locate it.

Something deep inside himself made him leave the camp that night.

Hope got ready to call it a night when she picked up her song coming back to her the same as two people humming. How would anyone know her song? This was impossible, this song belonged to her. Such strange feelings took place on this journey of a knowing of things to come, or connections with something that she felt deeply. She continued to process all of this.

As she listened to the melody, she experienced an energy connect with her. It was the strangest thing. Intrigued by this she continued to emanate light. When she heard and noticed it, the dog lifted his head like he sensed it too.

From the caves where Gracemama stayed, she watched. She watched Hope the whole time. It was not her job to intervene unless it affected her safety, a life or death event. She kept the men sleeping when the sun came up. She didn't know how long she could maintain this, but she would try. This was important. She needed to give this boy time to find Hope. She knew about him, but didn't perceive what was to come with him.

Finally, so tired, Hope crawled into her bed. She could barely keep her eyes open. The dog curled up next to her. She should make him a bed but she liked the warmth they shared, and when the fire died down during the night, she didn't get cold. She slept, and so did the dog. They had been up late, and unlike usual they slept into the morning.

The sun came up as the boy traveled. From time to time he stopped to study the trail. He ate some dried meat as he traveled; he realized he must keep going. At one point, he deliberately left the trail and walked for about an hour. He swept after walking off the trail a good long time. This trick he learned from the men. He tried to throw the hunters off by changing their direction. This should work if they got this far and hadn't turned back as they thought about the night before. If nothing else, it would give him time. He returned to the trail and continued sweeping to cover his tracks. It was a lot of work but important. These men were skilled trackers who he wanted to lose.

The men continued to sleep under Gracemama's spell. She hoped to keep them like this overnight or longer if possible. Whenever they woke, she hoped it would be morning, then they would not discover a day or more passed. She recognized they would realize the boy left. That part she couldn't do anything about.

Once back on the trail, the boy traveled for a while and picked up the sound of water. He rounded a bend still sweeping by dragging the branch. He came upon the waterfall, but didn't realize how close he was to Hope.

The boy dropped the branch once he arrived at the falls. He stopped, drank and splashed water on his face. Then he found footsteps all around the falls, small like the ones the men and he tracked. They led in a direction away from the falls, so he followed them and figured out he must be close. He understood he must be as quiet as possible. Hyper-vigilant he barely made a sound as he came close to Hope's little camp.

Hope slept deeply. The dog's head popped up. His eyes were wide open. He picked up the slightest noise a little way off. He licked Hope's face. Her eyes opened slowly. She lay there; it was daylight. How did she sleep so late? Then she heard it too. The sound was so low. What was it? Her body tensed as did the dog's. She gradually sat up making no sound. She kept her spear by her, and she picked it up. The sound came closer. It sounded like footsteps. Not many, just one. Was it an animal or a person? She would find out soon. It was close.

The boy had just about reached the mouth of the horseshoe opening. Hope stood in the ready. She had spread the gravel and the leaves, she would find out soon by the sound how close it was. The boy took one more step. There it was, the crunching sounds of dried leaves and gravel. The dog stood right at Hope's side. As it rounded the bend, she threw her spear. It nicked the boy's hip and then flew by. She grabbed her carving tool. The boy froze. The dog let out a low constant growl and ran forward at the Boy. Next, the dog put his teeth into the boy's wrist and the boy yelled in pain. Blood dripped through his pants from the spear and his wrist. The dog held his mouth on the boy's wrist.

Hope noticed that the boy carried no weapon. There was a spear tied to his pack, but anyone would carry a spear if they were away from other people on a journey or hunting. Her mind moved rapidly. He was a boy not a full grown man like her father. She yelled at the dog to stop. The dog lightened the pressure but did not let go. Hope thought quickly then she spoke. The dog stood his ground and did not move. He did not increase his bite. Hope saw blood from the boy. The boy did not advance and stood frozen. He made the choice not to have his weapon out. He wasn't sure why; it was an intuition. Now with an injury he wondered did he make the wrong decision? The boy experienced pain as he stood there.

Hope studied the boy. They locked eyes while they stood frozen to their spots. The boy couldn't move anyway. He seemed about her age. He had dark hair and eyes like Hope. As they stared at one another and studied each other, they both understood the connection. Not only did they connect, they seemed to travel through a memory from their youth. Their vision came together like a flash. They recognized one another as children at a young age. The two stood together in her village. They both asked the same question in their minds who was this person.

The boy fell down. The dog let go upon Hope's command. They shared an unspoken language or understanding already. He was hurt. Did she trust her gut? She believed she must. The instinct became strong. She needed to help him. Then she walked over to the boy. He had a small pool of blood near his hip where the spear had nicked him. He was weak. She took his legs and dragged him to her cave. She stoked the fire and heated water. The boy was out of it. The dog sat by alert and guarding. She laid the boy out. His arm would wait that was just a slight piercing from the dog's teeth. The other wound bled a lot where she hit him with her spear. She moved to her spot where she had unpacked all her healing herbs. The boy tried to speak, but she shushed him. He needed to let her work. He obeyed. Hope used all her knowledge. She cleaned the wound on his hip, then she dressed it with some herbs that would stop the bleeding and infection. She told him to be still and took care of his wrist. He had some small puncture wounds. They bled but not a lot. She cleaned them up and bandaged them. He tried to speak again, and she told him not to. She made broth and healing tea. He was so hungry at this point he was glad for it. The tea had a herb in it that would make him sleep. He did.

Hope asked herself some questions. Who was he? Where did he come from? Why did he seem familiar? She realized she recognized him, not now but from her past. She failed to put her finger on it. The dog stayed by her side and guarded her. After a while, she told the dog to guard the boy while she walked to the pool. Hope wanted to get fish and water. The dog obeyed. The girl returned with two fish, and she had replenished her water supply.

Hope cooked the fish now. The girl had become hungry and needed nourishment. Once cooked she ate. She would feed the dog and save the rest for when the boy woke up. The dog was hungry too and ate what she gave him. He did not eat the extra she saved for the boy. He understood. To her surprise, her trust and feelings were growing for him. Hope was amazed how the dog understood her and was glad for it. If she had been alone, she didn't know how this would have turned out. Dog helped protect her.

The boy slept for quite a while and then he stirred. The tea Hope gave him had helped him to sleep. He had exhausted himself from the trip. He moved and Hope watched him. She experienced this tug at her heart, and familiarity she couldn't place. The dog guarded the boy. His eyes opened. Reorienting himself took a minute. Then it came to him where he was. His body was sore. He moved his hand to his hip and pulled it back quickly. The boy remembered he had gotten injured; he had pain. His wrist was wrapped but didn't hurt as much as his hip. He was thankful Hope helped him and did not kill him. The dog might have harmed him if she hadn't called him off. He looked at Hope but didn't speak. He studied his surroundings. This little camp looked tidy and organized. He only saw one bed, so he assumed she lived here alone. Why would a girl of her age be alone in the wilderness like this? Strange, he thought. His gaze moved to Hope. She did not have a mean face. It looked kind, but he wouldn't misjudge it, she was quick and protective. As he looked at her, her face softened even more. They held each other's gaze. Then he studied the dog and thought *what a beautiful animal*. He appeared strong and powerful, but also something else. The fur looked thick and pure white, and the dog's eyes hypnotized. Without question the dog was protective of Hope. He did not stroke him. The boy closed his eyes and reflected in the quiet of his mind. He needed to talk to Hope, to feel her out and most likely warn her unless she showed another side or intention other than kindness. People could change quickly.

He opened his eyes and spoke, his voice weak. "My name is Kai. What is yours?" Hope didn't see a problem with telling him her name. "My name is Hope." And then she said, "I think you should eat," and offered him some fish. She fed him, and he gobbled the food down. He was still hungry. He drank water and then spoke again. Kai said, "I come to warn you. There are men coming after you. We saw your light and tracked you. I snuck away from the party to warn you. I walked off trail to disorient them in hopes they wouldn't pick up your trail again." "Why would you do that, why would you take that risk, I am nothing to you?" Hope asked. Kai answered, and it was not what she expected to hear. He said, "I saw your light, I experienced your light. It held much love. That's all I can tell you. I took a chance and trusted my instincts. I left the hunters by choice. It's unknown what they would do to you. Your light had a power and a feeling that is undeniable. Also I recognized it as familiar. I do not comprehend why. So I left and covered my tracks and tried to be smart about it. If they catch us, I do not know what will happen. I came to these men as a youth. I don't remember from where, but they are all I have known. Then your light shone, and I had this memory." Hope responded, "Me too."

Hope told the dog it was ok. The dog relaxed but would be quick if he needed to be. Kai thanked Hope for taking care of him, his wounds, and feeding him. "I should be on my way," Kai said. Hope told him he was too weak to travel yet, he needed to rest. She said she would make him some tea to help him rest. She did, he drank it and slept. The girl couldn't say why she had trust for Kai. She felt it in her gut. The boy was kind, and she was sorry they had injured him. At the time there was no other way to respond. She continued to wonder more about who he was.

The girl experienced pride to see the dog protect her like he had. She moved about cleaning up, she trusted the dog to continue to guard Kai, she left for the pool to wash up and ready for the day. She packed her pack in case she needed to flee. Hope didn't know if the men would show up and how far behind they were. She didn't realize Gracemama put a spell on them to gain her time. She confirmed to herself that she wouldn't leave Kai until he became stronger. The girl needed a plan. She would come up with one.

Hope thought she would send Kai away. He would only increase her danger, and it might put him in danger. She and the dog would go. The day had passed. Kai woke up one more time and she fed him, herself, and the dog and then he fell back to sleep. Hope finished organizing the camp and swept where she should so that no one would realize how long she had been there. The girl accepted it was time to leave at daybreak and would head back home. She hoped her timing was right.

She slept, and the dog lay by her side in her bed. When Kai had awoken earlier and eaten, she had made a makeshift ground cover with some of her needles, and he had a ground cloth. That way he would not get a chill. Hope got up at morning light. Kai was awake and sitting up. This surprised her. He had been thinking too. He thought if he traveled back to the hunters he might detain them or throw them off her track, or make up a good story. While he thought these thoughts, Hope prepared a hearty breakfast for all of them to use up the food. She supposed they would need the energy from the meal. Then she checked his wounds. They were both amazed. The herbs did their job better than expected. Kai still had cuts and such, he was a little sore, but nothing like he should be. Again he asked himself who this girl was.

The treatments Hope applied to the boy's wounds healed them up. She saw the amazing proprieties of these herbs and all she had learned. She snapped out of her thoughts. No time to daydream. She told Kai of her plan. She explained he would cover his injury on his hip and that he should unwrap his wrist before he caught up to the men and just explain an animal had attacked him. They both hoped the men wouldn't discover his other wound.

They shouldn't as long as he covered them well with his clothes. Once healed, he should bury the bandages. If he must explain it, he would say he got injured there at the same time. Yes, that should work. Hope hoped that Kai would be all right. Kai had concerns about her too. He knew nothing else about her or where she would go. He hated to leave her, but he needed to help her, and this was the only way. They both agreed this was the plan that was best. He explained how she would need to cover her trail, and she told him she had learned how. He took her hand unexpectedly and looked into her eyes. Kai had tears that surprised him. He thanked her for all she had done. She told him how brave he acted to warn her like he had. He had taken his life in his hands and took a big risk. She told him she hoped he would stay safe and hoped they would see each other again one day.

CHAPTER EIGHTEEN

Parting Ways

Kai and Hope parted ways. She decided to take the dog, no the dog decided to go with her, she laughed. Kai read her thoughts and laughed too. When they parted Hope and Kai hugged. They didn't even know one another, but there must be a reason they felt this connection. Oh well, they both dismissed it, time passed, and they both needed to get on their way. Both pushed their feelings aside and said goodbye. Hope did a good job of cleaning up the camp. It would be hard to discover someone lived there. The girl extinguished the fire and covered it over with dirt; she removed the surrounding rocks and all else she created. She hoped she made the right decision. Gracemama told her she would realize when to come home to her. She now recognized it was this present moment.

Hope headed back in the direction she came from. She took her branch and dragged it behind her. The dog walked by her side, this part of the trail was wide enough. She made good time. Hope wouldn't practice her light, for fear of being discovered again, she would keep it close. The girl would only use it when needed. She liked having the dog with her and wished Gracemama wouldn't be angry with her. Hope didn't remember others having any animals at the camp.

Kai traveled slower. Hope gave him some food to eat on the way so he wouldn't lose his strength. She gave him a dressing to apply midday, and that would be it. The wound healed so well she decided that would do it. Kai found his way but moved slowly. He realized that he was still a little weak. He stopped along the way when needed to change his dressings and eat. The boy realized he must stay alert, because if he ran into the men, he should have his story straight and no dressing on his wrist. He would hide the hip dressing. He saw his wounds healed; they looked good. Once again his questions came up about this girl. How did she learn all this at such a young age? Kai hated to part ways, but he did not have a choice. He hoped he would meet her again someday though he didn't see a way. He needed to protect her, and Kai saw no other way to accomplish that. The boy felt such a tug of his heart in the other direction. He understood they agreed, this was the only way, even though his heart said something else. Kai continued on his way. He was competent at following the trail. Once night fell, he found a place to sleep. His progress started slow, he was still healing. Kai awoke and ate food and left the camp as if he hadn't been there. He discarded and buried both bandages. This would help as he would have no trace of Hope on him. He kept a little food she gave him but discarded any other trace in the hole he dug and buried everything.

It was getting into the afternoon, Hope made good time. She remembered different markers along the way back. She stopped with the dog and ate a snack and closed her eyes for a short time. The dog licked her face to wake her up. They walked till just before the light faded. Hope found the marker from a camp she stayed at before. It would have supplies. She remembered where to dig and get the box and found it stocked with fresh supplies of tinder, porridge and a few other items. The box contained the same supplies as before. She realized this was intentional. Someone had traveled here to restock this place for her, and other travelers told about this location. This hidden location was safeguarded which helped her relax. The dog seemed a little more relaxed here too. Hope fixed the fire pit that was already there and readied it for a nice warm fire. She got it going with her flint and the beautiful lacy tinder from the supply box. The girl cooked up tasty porridge and then fed the dog. She didn't want to stop him from getting his own, so she didn't give him a lot. Hope admitted she liked caring for him. He was a good companion. She fixed her bedding and stared at the fire lost in thought, a luxury, but she seemed safe here. Darkness filled the air, but Hope couldn't sleep. The dog by her side, seemed more awake than usual. She soaked in the warmth from the fire. She remembered all the people she loved, her mother, her sister, her father. The possibility existed that darkness completely enveloped her father, but she hoped not. Hope thought of Gracemama, the camp and the women. The seven and now herself, she became a part of this group through Gracemama. She also recalled the rest of the people in the camp. Hope would be glad to return to Gracemama and the women.

After a long day Hope lay down to sleep and dream. Her mother and sister came to her. They said the time neared that she would return to them and fight the darkness. The darkness grew. Gracemama came to tell her she realized Hope headed back to her. She would wait in the cave. They would prepare for her trip back to her village. Gracemama told her she performed well. She gave her a warning to stay alert. Hope dreamed of many things through the night. She reviewed in her mind all she learned and then some. Additional teaching took place in her dreamtime. She didn't realize it, but Gracemama passed on more knowledge to her in her dream state. This was a huge undertaking for Hope. She grew up in every way during this time away from her village, and now she would need every trick and skill in the book. Gracemama disconnected and let Hope sleep with no thoughts or learning, just get rest. She slept and the dog by her side snuggled into her body.

Hope woke up, packed, spoke her morning prayers, thanks, and ate a morning meal. She left the camp and continued on her way. She tied the sweeping branch to a rope which she put on her waist to drag behind her, so she didn't have to carry it. It worked. No one would realize anyone stayed at the camp. Hope kept a good pace. She assumed she would make it back to Gracemama today if she kept alert and moved along. The dog often walked by her side. Sometimes as she walked, he left to scout the area. He never strayed too far, and they developed a way of communicating by now. Hope found if she even thought of him he would appear.

Hope found curious this tugging she continued to experience toward Kai. This impression stayed with her, but she pushed it to the back of her mind. She had other things to take care of. She wanted to get back to the caves by the end of tonight if possible. It was a reasonable expectation given where she had slept the previous night. She comprehended the distance. Hope passed the place she stopped at on her way out. She stopped briefly to eat by the water to fill her water container. She and the dog quenched their thirst. They did not stop long. She didn't want to rest. Confident of her strength Hope continued. The girl gained strength on her journey because of all the physical challenges. She petted the dog on the head as she walked; she loved this dog. He made a good companion, a good guard dog, and she sensed he would also protect her no matter what. She walked with enthusiasm at this point; she became excited to return as she got closer to her destination.

Back where the men slept with Gracemama's help, she believed the moment arrived to let the men wake up. She hoped for the best. One by one the men moved their bodies to wake up. A few men sat up and checked their surroundings. They didn't realize, as Gracemama hoped, that a few days passed since she woke them up in the morning; the men wouldn't notice, at least not right now. Each one of them knew the routine. They each took food out of their packs and ate. A few of them commented on how their hunger remained after eating. It was a small group. One of them noticed that Kai was not there. Where did he wander off to? Then he noticed his gear had disappeared too. He told the others right away. What was Kai up to? Where was he? Once they became aware and ate a little food, they all stood up. They must continue on their way. They couldn't wait for him; it looked like he left the camp. Otherwise, his belongings would have been there. They didn't say much because they had no answers. They started on their way, the way they headed before. The trackers looked to pick up the trail. They did not find it. That was strange. The men had some thoughts on why but weren't sure. They were not ones to jump to assumptions. The group continued in the direction anyway because it was a trail and a likely way someone would walk. After walking a good long way, they came across some footsteps small like the ones they tracked before. The steps headed off the trail; the group followed them. Eventually the footprints ended. The group wondered if they were deceived or what. They headed back up to the trail. This had taken them out of their way and wasted time. The men continued on, though they were not sure of the plan since there was nothing to follow, nothing to track. They gave it a while longer and if they didn't pick up a trail they needed to turn around and head home. The men agreed they spent too much time away from their camp. Now what they tracked was so far away from there it wouldn't be a danger. They were leaning toward heading home if something didn't happen soon.

Kai and the men were both advancing to a midpoint where they would soon meet. Kai expected this, they did not. A few hours into the morning, Kai pulled off by a creek near the path. Approaching, as he was taking a break, the boy heard the men's footsteps. Kai heard them speaking but could not determine who spoke. They were getting close. The boy ate the last of his food. He put on his pack and went back to the trail. Kai wanted to meet them and stop them from continuing. He was nervous but his desire to help Hope was stronger. The boy was committed.

As they came face to face, Kai was ready. He surprised the men. They both stopped and gazed at each other. Kai had readied his plan, he hoped it would work. The boy's first words were, "I found you, I expected you left me and went back to camp." The men said, "We figured you left us and maybe ran away. We weren't sure. We thought it strange." Kai talked. The boy said he lived with them so long and learned much, but he wanted to prove himself to them. He wanted them to be proud of him and told them he had left camp to scout the light. He wanted to show them he had learned well. Kai had turned back because he had not picked up a trail or found anything. He also told them an animal had injured him. That made him turn back. He showed them the wound on his wrist which was almost healed. He was convincing, and they believed him. They had pretty much decided to turn back by now.

His story held. They had nurtured him throughout his childhood. They did not expect he would just leave. Why, it made no sense. They talked for a while. Kai told them where he had gone and how far he walked, describing the terrain. He had his story well planned. The day before the men had talked about if they didn't pick up a trail they would turn back, now the group decided. They didn't consider the light or what it came from a threat any longer. They didn't think they needed to track it and waste any more time. There was plenty to do at the camp. Trusting Kai and his words, they decided the best thing to do was head back. Kai breathed a sigh of relief. It had worked. They knew his character. He felt bad deceiving them, but he figured out he had no choice but to implement this plan and his story. It did not cause harm to them, and it would help his new friend. That is how he thought of her now, with the deep connection and that he had met her somewhere before. There was no time to dwell on that, he needed to continue to regain the men's trust and stick to his story and get back to their camp as far away from Hope as possible. He took a big sigh of relief which no one noticed. But his mind wouldn't stop. Would he ever see her again? He didn't know. It weighed on him. He would rather have gone with her. He couldn't, not now. How would he ever find her again? The boy had to admit to himself as he headed out with the men, he experienced this quiet but steady tug on his heart continue. He needed to attend to the moment and drew himself back. He didn't need to ponder this now.

Hope and the dog continued on. The girl was happy to be heading back. She couldn't wait to see Gracemama. The dog was by her side most of the time. She had missed Gracemama, and all she embodied. Gracemama had been watching Hope's trip and progress the whole time. She had that ability to check in and see whenever she needed to. The Wise One knew how strong Hope had grown. She knew Hope was nearing the caves and would be glad to see her but also serious about what was to come.

CHAPTER NINETEEN

Return Journey

About dinner time, Hope came around a bend and arrived at the caves. She found Gracemama's cave, no one else was visible. The dog followed on her heels as she sped up. She motioned the dog to stay outside the cave door. She didn't want to address the subject of the dog yet. He obediently lay down and stayed there. Hope would beckon him when the time arrived. She walked into the cave, a soft light came from within. Gracemama sat near the fire waiting patiently. She stood up and opened her arms wide for a hug. Hope ran to her. She held her in the hug for a long time and Hope relaxed into it. Gracemama felt the shift. She had become a young woman now.

Hope experienced relief and happiness to be back. Slowly, Gracemama loosened her hug and let go of Hope. She stood back and gazed at her. Hope radiated light. After some time, Gracemama said to Hope, "You must be hungry, let's get some food." I have prepared a special meal for you. Gracemama spoke a prayer of thanks for the girl's safe return. Then they ate. The food tasted delicious or Hope was especially hungry or maybe both. Gracemama prepared a sweet tea at the end because this was a special occasion. The wise woman made a tea of sweet flowers, the girl took in the flavor and aroma. Gracemama worked at making this a special moment.

Silent while they ate their meals when Gracemama and Hope finished the two of them sipped their cups of tea and talked at length. Hope did not tell all the details, that would come over the next day or two, but she told her a general brief narrative about her trip. Gracemama was satisfied and learned more than Hope realized by monitoring the girl while she traveled. She didn't mention the dog yet or Kai. They sat together for a long time just enjoying each other's presence. Soon it would be time to sleep. The fire burned brightly. Nervous to tell Gracemama about the dog, Hope didn't know how to begin or how she would react. The girl couldn't bear at this point to part with him.

Suddenly, Gracemama clicked her tongue. Hope looked up surprised as they had been so quiet. The dog recognized this familiar sound and stood up and entered the cave. Hope stared at the dog and then looked at Gracemama. This was not her plan. She planned a long explanation about the dog and then would bring him in. The dog walked straight over to Gracemama. She hugged him and talked to him and ruffled his beautiful white fur. They stared at each other as if they recognized each other. The dog licked her cheek and then laid down between them. Shocked Hope didn't know what to think. How was this possible? Gracemama seemed to recognize the dog and the dog Gracemama. They seemed to be old friends. Hope couldn't speak. She didn't know what to say or ask. Gracemama began the conversation, "Hope meet Mechi my oldest friend and companion. When I was young like you, I had a teacher. Mechi was the same to my teacher. Mechi is older than you can imagine. A long time ago it was appropriate for Mechi to be with me; it was a similar time. A time when I both needed and earned a companion like him through the wisdom I gathered. He also spent time with your mother. He is now your companion. We pass him to you, and he knows this. He is wiser than all of us. He has lived a long time. We love him a great deal, now it is your turn. By no mistake he found you. He looked after you, guarding you, and let you learn." Hope was speechless. She thought she would tell Gracemama about this dog that showed up and ask if she might keep him. She planned, reviewed and practiced her speech she would deliver to Gracemama. Hope set herself up for success so that Gracemama would not say no. The tables unexpectedly turned. Mechi licked Hope's hand and held her gaze. He put his head on her lap as if to say I am with you now. Hope stroked his head and relaxed. Mechi comforted her through her confusion. Gracemama said to Hope, "Mechi will help you through the rest of your journey when you go to the village, he will be a great help."

Gracemama said, "Now it's time to sleep, we can talk more tomorrow. They both got ready to go to their sleeping spots; Mechi followed Hope. When she laid down, he rested in the curve of her body curled up in a ball. The three of them slept soundly. They both dreamt a lot. Gracemama carried a burden, and so did Hope. The girl understood the time approached that she would have to go home. Hope tossed and turned all night, she did not recall a restless sleep like this for a while. Gracemama felt somewhat unsettled and worried about Hope. This was an undertaking neither one of them had experienced. What would it entail to rid this town of darkness that ate away the light? Ravenous, the darkness would not stop. If her mother and her sister did not stay behind, the town would be dead by now. During the night, as she tossed and turned, her mother and sister both came to her. They came to her as if in a bubble in her dream and they calmed her. Hope calmed down with their words, and they told her they would stand with her. They reassured her it would all be all right, everything would be all right. As a group they would be strong and powerful standing together.

Tonight, Gracemama wrestled with the whole event about to take place. Her connection with Hope ran deep. She struggled with the fact of Hope going without her. The plan, Gracemama would stay behind and work from there. They needed someone left with her wisdom in case the others didn't make it. That became the reason for the decision that she would support them from afar. Gracemama received a visited from Hope's mother. They conversed in dreamtime about what was to come, and they made decisions that night. What calmed Gracemama is that she understood how powerful Hope's mother was.

Gracemama would only join them if no other choices existed and they were failing. Sometimes being there with the others would be more powerful, but she planned to work and help a lot from a distance for now. Hope's mother believed together they possessed the power they would require to overcome the darkness. Mechi would go along, and he possessed more power than all of them. Hope was unaware of his inner strength.

After a while, they settled in and slept the rest of the night. They even slept a little later than planned into the morning. It was necessary for them both to rest for what was coming. When they awoke, they prepared for the day. They looked at each other, locked their eyes, and gazed at each other for a long time. They got up and proceeded with their normal morning rituals of washing and dressing, then they would have food. Mechi stayed at Hope's spot for a while and then exited and wandered around nearby. When he returned, Hope and Gracemama ate a hearty breakfast. Mechi received a special meal too. The tea Gracemama made once again had a special purpose of propelling them into the day with power. They sat at the morning fire and talked. Hope still did not mention Kai though Gracemama knew about him. She didn't probe; she didn't think she needed to at the moment. They decided today they would spend together. The time to leave was near.

They would spend the day packing Hope up with all she needed. They emptied Hope's backpack out and started from scratch. What Hope would need for this trip differed from what she needed for the last trip. Next, they would lay everything out on the floor. Mechi would touch nothing. Gracemama moved to where the healing herbs were and picked through with care. She thought about what Hope might need for this journey. After she collected what she wanted the girl to have, she put everything in little bags she made. Then they went through the teas which possessed different properties. They too went into little bags. She created a way of

163

marking them so that Hope would identify what each bag contained. She made sure she had bandages for injuries just in case. Gracemama wished Hope wouldn't need any of this. Hope identified every item and what its purpose was. She understood Gracemama's intention for everything. There would be some salve, two different types. Next they packed things like clothes, food, and an eating bowl and utensils, and what she would need to sleep on and with. Hope could have done a lot of this herself, she had grown to the point of knowing, but it was a ritual and a way to spend their last day together. Gracemama rarely got emotional, but today with a lot of stirred up feelings she did. She struggled with not going and Hope leaving. Hope had a spot deep in Gracemama's heart, it was the most special of places.

Later in the day, they would go to the village and spend their last night there. She realized Hope would want to see the people of the village and the group of women and say goodbye in the morning before Hope and Mechi left. Once she left, Gracemama would return to the caves with her core group of women. Gracemama would guide them as to their part, she would watch over Hope and the others and assist in any way she could. No one knew how long this would take or how it would turn out. Gracemama believed she had given Hope all she needed. The girl possessed the knowledge and discipline and with her mother and sister and Mechi alongside they would be powerful. It was still an unknown result even though everyone had worked hard. She would do what she could and believed they had what it took to overcome this deep darkness Hope and the others would go into.

Hope had her moments on this day. It was that realization of what they would encounter, what was to come. It was an ominous task they were about to take on. There had never been darkness so deep that had taken over almost a whole village and its people. It was sucking the life-force out of everything. Did she have what it took?

After spending the day at the cave, Gracemama and Hope headed to her hut. They spent time in silence, praying, and then Gracemama pulled out a flute and played Hope's melody. It lifted Hope; she saw the light and the strength she had. The girl was ready for this. She had been learning and training, and with her mother, Sister and Mechi alongside, and Gracemama watching over them, she saw the vision. Hope saw they could do this. It wouldn't be easy, but they would do it.

After the melody, Mechi, who had been nearby all day, Gracemama, and Hope lay down and slept the most renewing sleep. Mother and Faith realized they were coming. They were anxious too, but in another way. Mother and Faith watched over the three as they slept. They were the ones that helped them rest so deeply.

The sun rose, and so did Hope, Gracemama, and Mechi. They prayed, got ready, and ate. Gracemama, Mechi, and Hope then stepped out of the hut. Everyone was there to see Hope off. Hope said her goodbyes. Gracemama walked Hope to the edge of the village. She hugged her and placed another special necklace around her for protection and to enhance her powers. Someone had given it to her, now it was for Hope. This was the third necklace Gracemama had given her. They all had special features in addition to or unique from the others. She wore them all. Now it was time to leave. Hope walked away from the village. The others stayed behind in the village. They were going about their day. Gracemama stood there at the edge of the village where she found Hope on the ground that first day. She stood there until Hope and Mechi were no longer in sight. Tears rolled down and off her cheeks. She recognized this would be the journey of Hope, the journey of her life.

The End.

ACKNOWLEDGEMENT

Foremost I want to thank my husband and my sons for their constant faith in me. My husband, Kevin's hard work ethic allowed me the time home to create the space to write this book. Without his support my writing and the completion of my book would not have been possible.

My oldest son David's friendship and steady encouragement in our conversations, phone calls, and visits checking up on me. He has become such a wise young man who watches out for others. His strength and courage is exceptional. Thank you for your love.

My youngest, Michael brought this publication and my website to fruition. We worked together for countless hours to create the actual physical manifestation of my written work. We laughed because we truly never realized what it took to embark on this project, my end of it (the writing and endless edits) or his role. He has guided me and stopped me from worries by advising me to take one step at a time was his motto. It has been a joy and a bonding in our relationship that surpasses what I imagined.

Though my parents are no longer living, I want to thank them because from my youngest years they believed in me.

My brothers Steven and David and their families, I hear your voices in my head of support and belief in whatever I take on which includes this book.

Sammie, my resident artist, thank you. You so thoughtfully put the cover together, creating a true piece of art that is the heart of my book. It is stunning and I love just looking at it. I had professional covers drawn and none of them came near to what you created for me.

Heartfelt thanks to my readers Sarah and Kayleen who gave constructive comments to improve my book You were invaluable and tough in checking my work in the early stages.

Thank you to my family and friends who have always been there in every way and supported me. You warm my heart. Words cannot express how important you are in my life.

Many thanks to my readers. My intention is to help others. My hope is this book provides inspiration in any way you need it, or just a good read. I don't know if I am good at this writing thing but will find out.

My sincere thanks to God every day for the blessed life I live and your constant guidance. I have been writing since I was a young girl and never realized this was so much a part of my soul's journey.

Hoping my readers understand that if you bring light and love to darkness, the light will be victorious. There is always Hope.

In Gratitude,

C.N. Jannain

30362904R00107

Made in the USA
San Bernardino, CA
25 March 2019